Looking f

Amanda Addison

Looking for Lucie

Amanda Addison

NEEM TREE
PRESS

Published by Neem Tree Press Limited, 2024

1 3 5 7 9 10 8 6 4 2

Neem Tree Press Limited
95A Ridgmount Gardens, London, WC1E 7AZ
United Kingdom
info@neemtreepress.com
www.neemtreepress.com

A catalogue record for this book is available from the British Library.

ISBN 978-1-911107-68-2 Paperback
ISBN 978-1-911107-69-9 Ebook

Printed and bound in Great Britain.

For Erin and Lawrence

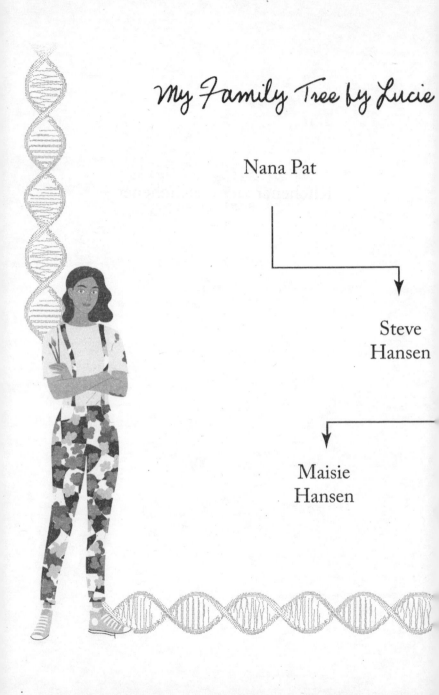

My Family Tree by Lucie

Nana Pat

Steve
Hansen

Maisie
Hansen

Hansen aged 8 and a half

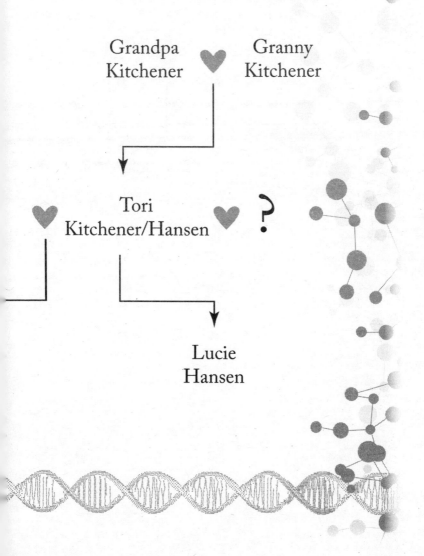

Grandpa
Kitchener 💜 Granny
Kitchener

Tori
Kitchener/Hansen 💜 ?

Lucie
Hansen

"The universe is one being. Everything and everyone is interconnected through an invisible web of stories. Whether we are aware of it or not, we are all in a silent conversation."

Shams of Tabriz

2016

Sunday 14ᵗʰ August

Lucie

Dad walks into the dining room carrying a showstopper of a cake. All eighteen candles flicker above the raspberry and pistachio topping.

"Happy birthday to you! Happy birthday to you! Happy birthday, dear Lucie. Happy birthday to you!" they sing.

"A work of art, Steve," says Nana Pat. "Remember when Maisie turned sixteen and you made an amazing gingerbread house."

"Baking is pretty similar to building: cake for bricks and cream for cement. Just on a much smaller scale!" laughs Dad.

Mum clears a space on the table. With a big inhale of breath, I blow out most of the candles.

"You can still make a wish," says Mum, as I extinguish the remaining candles.

I make my wish. Maisie nudges me. "What did you wish for?"

"It's a secret! If I tell you, it won't come true."

"Hey, Dad, you should go on Bake Off!" says Maisie.

My sister's right, Dad could win prizes for his cakes. He's used one of my textile designs. The pink and mint green

1

chequerboard pattern makes for an even more elaborate cake than the gingerbread house he made for Maisie. "Getting the repeat squares must have taken hours!"

"Patience and an eye for detail. Like tiling a bathroom," says Dad with a shrug.

"I filmed the whole thing," says Maisie. "I posted it online. People love baking videos!" The room goes silent whilst we all eat cake.

"It doesn't just look good; it tastes good too. The tangy raspberries and nuts are a perfect combination," says Mum pouring herself another glass of prosecco.

"Dad, this really is heavenly," I say. It tastes and smells so different from shop bought cakes. The raspberries smell of summer and the slightly burnt taste of the toasted pistachios against the moist sponge is so good. Dad could become a baker rather than a builder any day!

"Such creative talent! It runs in the family," says Nana Pat, sending a shiver down my spine. Dad and Nana aren't my blood relations. When I was a kid, Nana Pat and I always made my birthday cakes together and she'd tell me, "Lucie, you are following in my footsteps." Nana Pat is a brilliant crafter, too. Her hand embroidery is amazing. Until I became a teenager, she always made me a cross-stitch birthday card.

"What did you spend the money I gave you for studying so hard on?" asks Nana Pat.

"This and that," I say.

"Didn't you use it to buy art materials for uni?" asks Mum.

"Mostly," I reply, unable to tell any of them what I really spent the whole lot on. How do I tell them that comments

2

like "it runs in the family", really get to me sometimes? Sometimes there's no alternative but to spend money on a DNA test. It won't be long before the results are in.

Steve has been my dad since I was a toddler. However, he is blonde-haired and blue-eyed and Mum is a blue-eyed redhead. So, it's pretty obvious to everyone that he is my stepdad, because I, on the other hand, have mahogany brown hair and caramel skin. Whenever I meet new people, they always seem to ask me where I'm from. I always reply "Norfolk", but that isn't enough. Strangers want to know my biological father's origins, and ask, "Yes, but where are you *really* from?" I feel like an idiot not knowing.

"Steve, darling, is it time to drive Pat home?" says Mum.

In the hall Nana thrusts a twenty-pound note into my hand. "You already gave me money for my exams *and* my birthday!" I say.

"I know I shouldn't have favourites, but you've always been my favourite grandchild," she whispers.

I tear up.

"What's that all about?" she asks giving me a big hug.

I pull away. I'll never be able to tell Nana Pat, let alone my parents, about the DNA test.

"Tori, Maisie, we're off now," calls Dad.

Mum and Maisie come out of the kitchen, and we wave Dad and Nana Pat off. It's my birthday so for once I don't have to help clear up. Full of cake, I collapse on the sofa.

*

The day after my last exam, Nana Pat gave me fifty pounds for studying so hard. I spent it all on a special-offer DNA test which arrived a few days later in the post. *Did I really think this through?* The result has the possibility to change my life forever.

Hands trembling, I undid a cellophane package and took out the plastic tubes. *Was this how Maisie felt when she did that pregnancy test last summer?* It was so weird to see my younger sister do a pregnancy test. *That* could have been life changing too. I wasn't supposed to eat or drink before doing this. I broke the seal, carefully following the instructions as if doing a biology experiment. I suppose it was a sort of experiment, except this was nothing like the ones we did at school. This was personal. I was the guinea pig.

I spat into the tube several times before my saliva reached the marked line. All sealed in the prepaid envelope, I went downstairs, grabbed my denim jacket and popped the small package in my bag.

"Lucie!" Mum called. "Where are you going? You haven't had your breakfast."

Is Mum suspicious?

"I'm still full from dinner last night," I lied, my stomach rumbling. I was actually starving but I had more important things to think about than food. And I'm not one for skipping meals. When I abstained from chocolate for the whole forty days of Lent it was hell on Earth!

I touched the canvas pocket of my backpack, checking the package was still there. Mum loitered in the hall. She had been watching me, as if she knew I was up to something.

"I just need to pop to the shop," I told her, wondering if old Glynis in the village post office could be trusted to get such an important package into the right sack and off for processing.

"What's the rush? Oh, do you need some tampons?" Mum had whispered.

"No!" I had snapped. If only she knew the real reason that my cheeks were flushed and my heart pounding. If I had thought just a second more, I would have said yes to her question, just to get her off my back. Or, the explosive option: I could have opened my bag and said, "This is what is so important. This little package will tell me everything I never knew."

I headed out, letting the front door slam behind me.

*

That was six weeks ago. Now it is all about waiting for the results. Mum says she doesn't know anything about my biological father. She always tells me the same old story, that he was an anonymous sperm donor. I grab my phone from the coffee table and google "sperm donor". It's become a little ritual, something I do when questions flood my mind. I stare at the familiar words willing them to tell me something new.

> *Donor sperm can help you become pregnant, regardless of your sexuality, gender identity, or marital status.*
>
> *You can use sperm from an anonymous donor by going to a licensed fertility clinic. Sperm can also be donated by*

5

the donor directly to an intended recipient. These clinics may have their own stock of frozen donated sperm, or they may buy it in from a sperm bank. You may also be able to use sperm from abroad.

You can use a donor you already know—such as a friend, or a donor you have met through an introduction website.

Donor sperm can also be part of in vitro fertilisation (IVF) if necessary.

"Luce, what are you doing?" asks Maisie coming into the living room.

"Nothing." I quickly close the tab and change the conversation. "Can you send me the video of Dad making my cake? I want to share it."

Thursday 18th August

Lucie

I sit bolt upright in bed. There is a clanging noise. My first thought is: burglars or deer? Burglars. Because according to the neighbourhood watch posters, Reedby is the crime capital of the world. Apparently, thieves drive around the village in the middle of the night emptying sheds and garages of bikes, rowing machines and lawn mowers. That's probably because there are so many posh houses around here. Our chalet bungalow isn't one of them!

There are herds of muntjac deer living on the edge of the village. Mum says that though the deer look cute wandering around the garden, they are a nuisance. She's sore because they eat all her tulips. That isn't the worst problem in my opinion. When my friends from college were over for a barbecue, deer noises started from behind the hedge. The grunts and groans of mating deer are really loud and embarrassing. We cracked up all the way through eating our burgers.

"Just like the Wimbledon final," said my mate, Sam. "Grunts 'n' all!"

"That's the only entertainment you get around here!" I laughed, though it wasn't really a joke.

7

I creep over to the window. Pitch dark. It must be cloudy as there's no moon and no stars. There is also no revving of engines or grunting of bucks. Only the deafening silence of living in the countryside. The noise must have been a shed door banging. Nothing interesting ever happens here. This is why I want to go to art school in London and live the 24/7 life where buses don't stop at teatime and bars and cafes are open until the early hours. There is another reason I want to leave too. I've never felt that I fit in here; I don't look the part, not the way Mum, Dad and Maisie do. In a big city there are other people who look just like me.

I check the time. 2.47am, Thursday 18th August. I always think of the colour orange when anyone says Thursday, but today all I can think is: *Results Day*.

I need to go back to sleep, but I am tempted to check my messages and see if anyone else is awake. I also really want to check my emails to see if the DNA results have come through. I've heard that these kinds of automated emails can arrive in the middle of the night. But I am really strict with myself, no phone after midnight, just like when I was doing my exams. I need to go back to sleep, otherwise I'll never wake up in time to catch the bus into college and collect my A-level results.

I toss and turn wondering why I am being so hard on myself. Maisie would just stay up all night sending messages and then sleep all day. "Lucie, the sensible one", everyone always says.

Ever since I was little, I've had a brilliant way of getting back to sleep. I tell myself these stories where I'm the main character. They're always about me and my real dad and take place in some faraway location. I've played them out in my head for years.

Tonight, I am setting my story in Spain. We once met a Spanish family at the village pub on the river. The wife, who'd been gazing at me for a while, finally came over to our table. Our fish and chips had just arrived after an hour's wait. I assumed she was going to ask Mum and Dad why the food was taking so long. She looked at our food. Then she looked at me. "You look exactly like a girl I know in Granada," she said. "Do you know Iñes Costa? Could you be her sister, or cousin?"

I shook my head.

"You do look a bit Spanish," said Maisie. Mum and Dad looked down at their dinner; as if embarrassed by my very presence. Luckily, the woman's husband called her back—their dinner had finally arrived.

Afterwards, I googled Granada. It's a beautiful city in the south of Spain between mountains and sea and most famous for the Alhambra Palace. The Moorish patterns, all geometric sweeps and swirls are amazing. They inspired some of my textile designs for my art assignments. Will the DNA test results include the south of Spain, I wonder? I play the story in my head. Set in Granada, I play the leading role where I am the daughter of a famous artist.

*

According to Mum #ALevelResultsDay is trending on Twitter. Both Mum and Dad are offering to give me a lift into town but I prefer to make my own way to college, even if I am tired. I don't like having an audience; I especially don't like having my parents in the audience! Nevertheless, I carefully choose a pair of patterned pantaloon trousers and a black strappy sun top. Mum says my new trainers clash with the trousers, but I think they complement them.

There's already a crowd at the village green waiting for the bus into town. The grass is still damp after last night's downpour, so I sit on my backpack. There's a fresh smell in the air that you don't get in the city. I wait alongside the pensioners and a couple of Eastern Europeans who work at Green Valley Farm.

A tall blonde girl looks down at me and says, "In our country we have a saying that before every important journey you sit on your bag, and—what's the word…? Contemplate. Yes, you contemplate."

I look up and smile. "It's kind of an important journey."

"Where are you from?" she asks.

Here we go again. I could say, "I've lived in this village since I was a few months old," but it's not what she means. It's always the same question, "Where are you from?" If I answer truthfully, the next question comes in close succession, "But where are you *really* from?" That gets me every time, makes me wonder if I really belong anywhere. I've rehearsed a new answer to the question. I will say, "The real question to ask is: where are you going?" I take a few deep breaths and am about to try this out when the yellow bus hurtles down the far edge of the green and everyone readies themselves for the journey.

There's an empty seat at the back. I connect with the bus's free WiFi and check my phone. A whole load of *good luck with your A-levels* messages. Nothing from the DNA test. It's been nearly six weeks since I posted it. The results must be arriving soon. I panic for a moment. What if the A-level and the DNA results do both come today? Two life changing results all in one day!

The walk from the bus station is busy. I look out for a familiar face. Why does Jenny have to be on holiday? Today of all days! We'd have gone for a drink together after the results, however well or badly we'd both done. It's alright for Jenny, she's so brilliant she already has an unconditional offer from Camberwell School of Art in London, so it doesn't matter what her results are. My art school offer is conditional on my grades. My whole future hangs in the balance. *Stop being so melodramatic!* I tell myself all the while checking my phone for messages from Jenny. It's an hour ahead in Brittany where she is staying in a remote cottage without any WiFi and only a very occasional phone signal. My phone buzzes, finally, a message from her.

Jenny: Results???

Lucie: On my way to college now.

A sinking sensation pulls at my stomach and my legs turn to jelly. I wish I was with Jenny and her family having fun on the beach: eating croissants, swimming and surfing. I can't actually surf—Jenny's older brother Matt is an amazing surfer—I'd be happy just watching. Anywhere, rather than here, collecting my results without my best friend.

To distract myself from the rising panic I practise some mindfulness. *Focus on your breathing. What can you see, hear and smell right now?* I can almost hear Natalie, my art tutor's voice guiding me. I walk slowly. Mindfully. I gaze up at the horse chestnut tree and zone in on the orange and golden-brown leaves. Bold silhouettes, cut out like Matisse stencils against the solid blue sky.

Something brushes past me. "Watch where you're going!" says a girl clutching the lead of her black dog. They overtake me on the corner and head up the steps in to college.

The smell of drying paint hits me first. They've decorated the ground floor corridor over the holidays. I'm not sure about the choice of lime green. It just adds to the tightening of my stomach and general wobbly feeling. Decisions. *Do I go to the art studio first and collect my portfolio, or continue to the top floor for the results?*

The studio is unrecognisable. It has been transformed into a clean and tidy space—ready for the start of term. There's a strong smell of white emulsion paint. No physical evidence that Jenny and I, or any of the other students were ever here, except that is, for a display of portraits we made in the first week. The induction project was to take a famous portrait and turn it into a meme. The captioned images could be funny, insulting, or both. Natalie told us that the term meme was invented by Richard Dawkins, an expert on genetics. It comes from the Ancient Greek word for imitate, μιμέομαι, i.e., *mimeomai*. We learnt how memes are like the genes in DNA that enable life-forms to multiply and spread around the world. Looking back, I wonder if that lesson sowed the seed of me thinking about taking a DNA test.

Natalie is pinning up pictures based on ones by famous artists: Van Gogh, Rembrandt, Leonardo da Vinci. These are what Natalie calls "DWEMS" (dead, white, European males). Most of my classmates chose these artists that everyone has heard of. They are usually the answer to any generic art questions in a pub quiz. She adds pictures inspired by contemporary artists: Jenny Saville, Tracey Emin, Marc Quinn and Chris Ofili.

Jenny had painted in a perfect imitation of Leonardo's style: the brush work, the pose, the enigmatic smile, wearing a brown dress which showed off her cleavage and long brown hair. If you were playing spot-the-difference you couldn't fail to notice the one crucial disparity. Jenny's *Mona Lisa* was having a very bad hair day, so she'd captioned it *Monday Lisa*. We were all amazed when Jenny's *Monday Lisa* went viral. Jenny had used some new products on her hair that morning which promised a natural look, but instead she ended up with a wild look. She'd painted her hair just as it was. When she posted the painting to her art account on Instagram she captioned it #MondayLisa, as if she'd just rolled out of bed and into college in a mad rush. The local television news came to the art studio and filmed her beside the portrait!

"Hi Natalie," I say.

"Lucie, good to see you," she replies, smiling as she adds a final famous picture. A self-portrait by Frida Kahlo. This is the picture I used as inspiration for my painting. Frida's don't-mess-with-me face is framed by brightly painted birds and flowers. I love the bold and vibrant colours in this painting. Frida was renowned for her colourful wardrobe: a combination of traditional Mexican folk designs and fashion from Europe. She is my style icon. Her eclectic taste and love of colour, print and pattern really speaks to me; reminds me of picking up interesting clothes in charity shops. Even stars like Beyoncé and Doja Cat have cited her as a fashion icon!

And what's more, Frida's face is so much more intriguing than the Mona Lisa's. Especially as her long, dark hair and striking eyebrows are rather like mine. It was the first time I'd seen someone who looked like me in a famous painting.

"Good timing," says Natalie as she finishes pinning my painting on the wall. I cringe thinking back to the first year of A-levels and how I thought my meme was the best piece of artwork in the class. To be honest I was miffed that it didn't get as many likes as Jenny's *Monday Lisa*. Now I can see why! I was more interested in designing my own swirly floral patterns to frame the face than coming up with a cool concept. I ended up captioning it: *Never apologise for a selfie*.

Natalie gets down carefully from the stepladder. She is petite, with mid-length auburn hair and dressed in black trousers, Doc Martins and a print tunic. I've always found her similarity to my mother uncanny. *Maybe we are related? That would be cool!*

"How did you do?" Natalie asks.

Doesn't Natalie already know? She's the one who marked our work. "I haven't been up there yet. Thought I'd get my folder first."

"Sure. They're all on the shelf, Lucie. Good luck! Your art exam went well," she adds climbing back on the ladder.

"Thanks," I say, slipping my phone into my free hand and grabbing the portfolio with my name. It's a lot heavier than I remembered.

By the time I reach the third floor, my new floral Nikes are pinching my toes and my portfolio is killing my arm. The corridor is U-shaped with paper signs on each door. A-G, H-L, M-R, S-Z... I look for H for Hansen. The H-L room is at the far end.

I head slowly down the corridor, looking at my phone. From the corner of my eye I see a silhouette marching purposefully in my direction. They are clutching their results envelope and talking into their phone, completely unaware of anyone else. They're heading straight for me.

"Look out!" I shout as I try swerving to the left, but we veer in the same direction. We collide. And, as if in slow motion, my phone drops out of my hand.

Nav

We fall over her portfolio. I reach out to catch her phone but miss it by millimetres. It plunges to the floor. *Please don't break!* I am feeling guilty already. This collision is entirely my fault.

"It's wrecked!" she gasps.

I hang up from my call and scramble for her phone. On my hands and knees, I run my fingers across the cracked screen. I try the on/off button.

Nothing.

"Are *you* okay?" I ask.

"You should look where you're going!" she snaps. Our eyes meet. Hers begin to well up and she turns away, embarrassed. But it isn't the almost-teary eyes which knock me off balance for a second time in as many minutes. There's something familiar about her, although I'm sure we've never met.

"It's got all my photographs on it. I don't mean just pictures of me and my friends. It has photos of my artwork."

"I can mend it," I say, looking at the broken screen. It doesn't look any worse than the ones I fix in the shop I sometimes help out at.

"I doubt you can."

"Will you let me try?" I plead.

We stand up.

She takes a deep breath and nods. "Wait here with my stuff whilst I get my results," she says. "Don't let my portfolio out of your sight!"

I prop her black portfolio case against the wall. It weighs a tonne! What on earth is in it? A flattened out dead body? Having a GP for a father and doing Biology A-level leads your mind down surprising paths.

Daniel Adams, the vice principal, and a hipster bearded guy with a camera make their way down the corridor. *Did he see the collision? Is he going to tell me to get the girl a new phone?* I could do that, but it won't save her photos.

"I'm glad I've caught you," says Mr Adams, stopping to speak to me. He doesn't look quite himself out of his usual navy suit and bright white shirt. The beige chinos and check shirt look weird—like he's stolen my father's work clothes.

"This is Stefan from the *East Anglian Evening Times*," he says turning to the bearded man. "They're looking to write a feature and take a photograph of students with their results out on the lawn. And we know how well you've done, Nav." He pats me on the shoulder.

The photographer smiles as if he knows me and it's a done deal.

"Sure," I say. I'm used to being headhunted for photo shoots and open days. It's not my excellent grades which make me so sought after. The unspeakable truth is they only want to photograph me because I have dark hair, dark eyes and brown skin. All of which, at this college, in this town, is a rarity. But I can't help wonder, how far would they really go to make everyone feel welcome? Or are they just cynically ticking some diversity box to make themselves feel good?

"Excellent. Good man," says the vice principal. "Lesley and Sally are downstairs too," he adds, breezily.

Of course, you've got Lesley and Sally! We're already on the cover of next year's prospectus too. Lesley Reynolds was in my maths class and is visually impaired. She takes Sally, her black Labrador guide dog, everywhere. I guess Amina isn't around for a photo or else she would have been summoned too. Most likely she made a quick exit to go and play volleyball.

"I have to stay here with this portfolio for a few minutes, until its owner gets back."

"No problem. We can wait," says Mr Adams.

There's an awkward silence which Mr Adams and the photographer fill by talking about the weather. Why do older people do that? I fill my time by doing something useful;

I look for the girl's name and contact details on the side of the portfolio. Nothing. I'd like to peek inside and check, but best not. I don't want to damage anything else of hers. She exits the results room and she's smiling.

"Got what I needed!" she says enigmatically, waving the envelope in the air.

"How did you get on?" asks Mr Adams.

Why didn't I ask first? I'm desperate to redeem myself for earlier—today is supposed to be a good day.

"Three A grades, including an A* for Art. Art school here I come!"

"Most deserved," says Mr Adams.

She takes the handles of her portfolio, darting me a short, sharp smile. "Alright?" she asks.

"Yeah," I mumble. "Thanks for asking."

Mr Adams looks thoughtful for a moment as if deliberating something important. He says to her, "You must join us for the photo shoot."

I don't like to be cynical, but I find myself sniggering. *Must be Mr Adams' lucky day*, I think. *Not one, but two brown kids to go with the blind girl—an inclusion and diversity optics full house.* Although lighter and fairer than me, she is still brown, a milky coffee brown; as white people tend to describe us. They love to describe people of colour in terms of coffee or chocolate.

"You can represent the arts, and young Nav here, the sciences."

So apparently that's the reason they've chosen us.

"Nav lives for science. Don't you?" adds Mr Adams.

I cringe. I just like science. I don't understand why most people aren't as curious as me about the world and how things work. To be honest, most of what I've learnt is from watching YouTube tutorials in my spare time, rather than what I've learnt in class.

The photographer points to the portfolio and suggests that she hold up a piece of artwork for the shoot.

"Okay," she says cautiously.

"It's Lucie, isn't it?" asks Mr Adams.

She nods.

So, she's Lucie. She doesn't look like a Lucie. More an Aisha, Leila, Yasmin.

Mr Adams prides himself on knowing people's names. I wonder if he sits at home with pages of names and photos and gets his wife to test him. I could do that if I wanted to. My brain works like that. But I'm learning not to be too public about memorising things. When I was a kid people liked it. I had all sorts of party tricks. I knew (and can still recall) the capital cities of every country, and won the county Spelling Bee. Now I'm seventeen, people think you're weird if you show off about these things too much.

"We need to get going," says the photographer.

"Absolutely," says Mr Adams. "Nav, Lucie, shall we?"

Lucie

It shows just how big the college is that after being here for two years, I am about to be photographed with students I have only just met. Unlike my high school where everyone knew everyone, and their parents too!

I stand next to Lesley and her dog Sally. Sally is wearing a Dayglo green harness and panting loudly, and what's more, her saliva is dribbling onto my new trainers! I step aside and turn to Lesley, who like a celebrity, is wearing dark glasses. *Does she know that her black Labrador is slobbering everywhere? Do I tell her?*

"Lesley, can you see your dog?" I ask. *What a stupid thing to say!* Maisie would have been able to say the right thing. If my sister had a superpower, it is that. She has a knack for asking the right questions and saying the things everyone is thinking, but she can do it without causing offence. People tell her all kinds of personal things. She'd make a brilliant journalist.

"I see a kind of blurry halo of people and shapes," replies Lesley. "Sally has her own particular shape. My mum says she resembles an upturned beer barrel. Too fond of her treats!"

"Ah, cute," I say suddenly feeling a lot less annoyed about my slobbered-on trainers.

"Thanks for asking," says Lesley, still facing forward.

She wasn't offended after all!

"People assume I can't see anything. They think everyone is either blind or sighted. The world isn't binary. Most of us are somewhere in between."

"You're so right." Now I want to ask her so many things. All kinds of questions flit through my mind: *How do you use social media if you're blind? How do you put make-up on? Can you tell more about a person from their voice? They say when you lose one sense, the others become heightened. Is that true?* As my mind whirrs, I suddenly remember all the ignorant questions people have asked me all my life. I decide to keep quiet.

I remember Maisie telling me about Molly someone or other, who is visually impaired and is a really popular YouTuber. I'm making a mental note to look her up later when the photographer starts giving us instructions.

"Stand a little closer please," says the photographer.

We all nudge in.

A tall guy in Lycra shorts and a T-shirt with the college logo splashed across the front stands behind us. He has to be one of the Sports Science students collecting his results. He's a walking advertisement for the college, with *Anything's Possible* in big letters across his broad chest. I wonder if he deliberately wore it so he'd get his photo taken. But then again, all the sport students seem to love uniforms. I can feel his damp, sweaty T-shirt touch my back and his clammy breath on my neck. I move to the side.

"And another one with you holding up your artwork. The one we agreed on. With the red and gold circle pattern," says the photographer.

I hold it up in front of me. My eyes peep over the fabric which conveniently hides most of my face. I prefer my fabric design being in the photograph than me.

"Lower it down, so we can see your lovely face," says the photographer. Obediently, I lower the fabric design to my neckline. My eyes meet the photographer's and I smile in silent reply. *Why did I do that?* Would he say to the sports student, "Let's see your lovely muscles!"? I don't know. Anyway, I guess it now looks like a design for a top.

"That's better. It looked like you were wearing a veil!"

Mr Adams sighs and shakes his head imperceptibly, but he doesn't say a word. *Is he thinking what I'm thinking?* My thoughts run down a familiar path. Just because I'm female with caramel-coloured skin holding fabric in front of my face, this photographer's mind has leapt to a very stereotypical place. It doesn't even make sense! When I've seen women in London wearing hijabs with veils, they are always plain colours—nothing so bright and patterned as my design.

Would the photographer say the veil thing to *anyone* holding a piece of fabric up? And isn't that offensive? Perhaps I *am* descended from a long line of Muslims, or even Jews or Hindus. Who knows what I'll discover. I can't help but wonder which results will change my life most, A-levels or the DNA test? I want to check the test results when this photo shoot is over, but I can't. I no longer have a functioning phone and my laptop is at home.

"And one more shot with the principal."

"Vice principal," says Mr Adams edging in beside us.

"Perfect! I'll get all the details from you, and with any luck, you'll be in tonight's *East Anglian Evening Times*," says the photographer smiling.

The sports student jogs off to the football pitch and Lesley and the dog are gone. "Stefan, we're looking forward to seeing our college name in the headlines," says Mr Adams.

"Me too," says Stefan, rolling up his sleeves and packing his camera equipment away.

It's then that I see the eye of Horus tattoo on his forearm. I recognise the two black lines outlining an eye, and inside it a black circle. The image is finished off with a further sweeping thick line for the eyebrow. I can't stop myself from staring. After all it is his trademark. It is so cool to use the Ancient

22

Egyptian Horus eye as a tattoo image. It means all-seeing. How perfect for a photographer! I suddenly feel nervous and in awe. I swallow hard before speaking.

"Are you *the* Stefan Lasky aka Horus? The one who took the famous photograph of the beggar in the doorway of that boarded-up department store in the city?" I ask.

"Yes, it was me," he says.

"The one that went viral?" asks Nav, his eyes widening.

"Yup. The headline: *City Beggars Face Ban* was down to me."

"My mum says that photograph is an icon of the twenty-first century. She loved it! She's a photographer too."

Stefan (aka Horus) smiles and rubs his beard a little embarrassed by the praise. "Mum says photographers were well paid in the pre-digital age. There was so much work about before we all had cameras on our phones."

"So true. The image may have gone viral and hit all the main news outlets, but I've seen very little in the way of extra income. I have fame but not fortune," laughs Stefan.

"My mum says that's because people don't value the arts. They expect everything for free."

"Absolutely," says Stefan. "What does your mum photograph?"

Is he just being polite asking about Mum's photographs? He probably assumes that she is an amateur photographer who has thousands of boring photographs stored on her phone and with the click of a button sends them to the newspaper with the hope of seeing herself in print. So I make sure to set him straight and say, "She used to travel the world photographing people and places for magazines."

"Cool," says Stefan.

"She's not a proper photographer anymore, she just lectures in it."

Mr Adams, "Stefan, let's go up to my office. I'll make sure you've got all the correct details about these youngsters."

Nav

We are standing on the steps by the entrance. The others have gone. "I'll get your phone sorted as quickly as I can," I say, looking at my feet. I'm struggling to look her in the face. There's still something about her that I can't quite figure out.

"What if you can't mend it?"

"I'm pretty good at fixing tech. Nothing's impossible," I say, forcing myself to look up at her.

"Of course, things are impossible," she snaps. "Or do you actually believe that *Anything's Possible?*"

This is the college motto, the one in big red letters on college hoodies. I don't believe it in the warm and cuddly way Mr Adams talks about it, but it's still an exciting concept. "In theory there are always infinite possibilities. It just might not be in the way you're expecting. There's scientific evidence to support this. Genetics is a prime example."

She rolls her eyes. "Really? You don't say."

Oh no! I've gone full science-talk again. "Green eyes are the rarest," I say, thinking that a reference to a feature of her own might be more interesting to her.

"What's that got to do with anything?" she asks.

"It is an interesting scientific fact that only 2% of the world's population has green eyes. Green eye-colour is the result of a mild amount of pigmentation in the eye with a golden tint. The gene that's responsible for this is called OCA2, and it controls melanin. Originally all humans had brown eyes with lots of melanin pigment. To put it simply, one day a nearby gene mutated and started to limit OCA2's ability to produce melanin in the iris."

She's frowning. I've gone on too much! I thought Lucie might be interested in these kinds of observations. Especially about colour, being as she's an artist. Artists are like scientists; they notice things that most other people fail to see. That's what I thought, anyway.

'Is it possible for parents with blue eyes to have a brown or green-eyed child?" she asks.

"Sure and vice versa. What colour are your parents' eyes?" I ask.

She hesitates and looks down at her feet.

That's odd, this isn't a trick question.

She steadies her hand on her portfolio.

"Blue and…" she pauses.

There's a long silence.

I realise I don't actually need the information to answer her. "Okay. Well, from what scientists now know, it isn't just the parents' eye colour which determines a child with green eyes. You have to go further back. What we do know is that there is no set formula."

She shrugs.

I can't make out whether she's interested in this or not. She looks annoyed. Or maybe more upset than annoyed. Why would someone be upset about eye colour? It's 100% nature.

It's not like height, where environmental factors—nurture—play a part. Sometimes I just don't get people.

"It's like me being considerably taller than my parents," I continue. "There are nearly seven hundred genetic variants which determine height. Plus, your diet. This makes for innumerable—"

"Can we talk about this subject another day?" Lucie interrupts.

"Sure." Does this mean she wants to see me again? Could I really become friends with a cool girl like her? Oh, but wait a minute. It's all about the phone. Seeing me again is all about the phone. Of course.

"Do you have a landline number so I can call when your phone's mended?" I ask, keeping the conversation strictly business.

Lucie rummages in her portfolio and takes out a sketchbook. She rapidly flicks through pages of drawings.

"Those look familiar," I say noting the swirly geometric patterns.

"They are original." She sounds touchy about it.

"I didn't mean they weren't." *Why is it so hard to say the right thing?* I guess I've always been scared of the arts and humanities because you have to have a clever opinion. And people say maths and science are hard! They are so much more straightforward any day.

"Actually, the Alhambra palace in Spain was my inspiration for these designs."

"Islamic patterns," I say.

"Exactly," she says almost breaking into a smile. She finds a blank sheet of paper, scribbles her home number and rips out the page.

"You don't live in town, then?" I ask reading the south Norfolk area code.

"No, I don't. I'd better go and get the bus. There's only a few a day." She picks up the portfolio.

It's now or never. Why is it so hard to say things that I could easily type in a text message? Sometimes saying the right thing to a stranger seems a whole load harder than sitting exams. Thank God you don't get tested in that! My UCAS score would have been nil points.

"Do you want a hand with that into town?" I ask looking at the portfolio. There's a pause. *Have I said the wrong thing again? Will she think I'm being sexist offering to carry it?* This folder is considerably heavier and more awkward than a pile of textbooks. I am almost six foot and I'd estimate she's almost a foot shorter.

"It's...umm...it's a simple matter of height...not just weight." I stumble over my words in an attempt to fill the silence.

"Weight?" she asks horrified.

"Not *your* weight," I explain. "The *portfolio* is heavy, and it would be well off the floor if I carried it. It wouldn't drag on the pavement and get damaged."

"Sure. Be my guest."

I pick up the folder and we walk together down the road. There's already some conkers on the pavement and part of me wants to step on their Dayglo green shells. But I don't in case she thinks I'm being childish. It's a shame they'll never make it to mature full-grown shells which house big shiny conkers. Best not tell her that I used to love playing conkers—still do. She'll definitely think I'm immature. Instead I say, "Did you know there are so many variants which cause one conker to reach maturity and another to come to nothing?"

She's smiling now. "That's so interesting. I've never thought of that."

"Really?"

"Yeah. I'm not being sarcastic; I was looking at the conkers too. My friends never say things like that. They're usually too interested in talking about themselves to notice what's going on around them."

Her eyes look bigger when she smiles and they shine a Dayglo green the colour of the conker shells. They're shaped like cat's eyes. I'm so sure I have never seen her around college, and yet she seems so familiar.

*

We wander down the slope into the shade of the underpass. I don't know what to make of Nav. I've never met anyone quite like him before. I've always hung out with the arts and humanities crowd. He seems different to them, and I don't want to turn right for the bus station and head straight home.

The walls are lined with murals, each one different to the one next to it. "Our whole art class did these!" I tell him. "We painted our pictures onto hardboard in the studio and the college installed them—apparently the risk assessment didn't cover us to paint them here, out in the real world!"

The humid smell of pee and chlorine is gross, just like the changing areas at a grotty public swimming pool. No wonder the college thought a whole day painting here in the subway was a health and safety nightmare!

"I've never really noticed the murals," says Nav gazing across at them. To an outsider, they must look like a bizarre collection of images: the scary super-size cat portrait, graffiti style geometric and swirly patterns, people with pound signs for eyes, urban buildings against the cathedral spire. Something for everyone!

"Don't you walk past them every time you go from college into town?"

"I do, but I've usually got something going on in my head. Things I'm working out," says Nav.

"Guess which one's mine?" I ask. He steps back from the murals. "Something colourful?"

"Getting warm, but which one?"

He gravitates towards Jenny's mural of celebrities, big, bold slabs of colour outlined in black. The use of jagged and overlapping Picasso style shapes is so clever. *Please don't choose hers!* Jenny is my best friend *and* an amazing artist. But people always like her work more than mine.

"Is it this one?"

I shake my head.

"Do I get another guess? Or do I have to wait until next time we come this way?" asks Nav.

"I'm not sure there'll be a next time. We've left college," I point out.

"I guess you're right. But I do notice things. Different things," says Nav. "For example, can you hear that?"

"Hear what?"

29

"The singing, coming from down there at the end of the underpass," he replies.

The scrawny busker really does resemble his dog—a greyhound or whippet, perhaps? He is singing a David Bowie number and strums along on his guitar. How come I never paid attention to any of the buskers before? Probably because I was always too busy watching people's reactions to the murals.

"He's always here," says Nav, searching in his wallet. He tosses a few coins into the tattered baseball cap. The busker nods. I follow suit, still wondering how I've never really noticed him before. I certainly haven't thought to give him any money! Why didn't I ever give him any change? We stop for a moment and wait for the end of "Changes".

The song sends a shiver down my spine. I've never really paid attention to the words. But today the lyrics "I can't trace time" just makes me think about looking back to where I came from and my DNA test.

"Are you okay?" asks Nav.

"I'm good," I say. Part of me feels like telling Nav about my search for my heritage, but I hardly know him. What's more, there's something I really like about being around Nav. Not in a romantic sense, but there's something easy and comfortable about hanging out with him. Something familiar, almost.

"My dad plays this track," says Nav.

"Really? So does mine. Bowie is pretty timeless, don't you think?"

"Yeah. Dad actually has the original 1970s *Hunky Dory* album on vinyl."

"Cool," I say. "My dad just plays it on YouTube. He's too much of a cost-cutter to subscribe to Spotify!"

The song finishes and we walk on. I wonder if my biological father listens to Bowie too.

"Did you know Bowie had two different coloured eyes?" I say, thinking about what Nav said about green eyes.

"No, Bowie's irises were the same colour," says Nav. "One iris was bigger than the other and that made them appear to be different colours."

I laugh. "Is there anything you don't know?" I tease, giving him a shove. An image of the artist Marc Quinn's gigantic photographs of irises—the Mesosphere series I saw at the Saatchi Gallery —pops into my head. "Have you seen Marc Quinn's Mesosphere pictures?" I ask.

"Mesospheres? From Bowie to mesospheres. That's some jump!"

"I was thinking about what you said earlier about eyes," I explain.

"That doesn't make sense. Isn't the mesosphere the layer of the earth's atmosphere that's directly above the stratosphere?" replies Nav, brow furrowed.

My God! How does he know all that? "These mesospheres are the most amazing paintings of irises," I explain. "The Mesosphere series of screen printed digital prints were taken of Quinn's paintings with a special close-up lens."

"The iris is the only internal organ you can see from the outside," says Nav.

"Right, so you'll like this. The artist's original 2009 Iris paintings were subtitled: *We share our chemistry with the stars*."

"Cool," says Nav.

Have I been talking too much? It's not the sort of thing I normally mention outside of an art class. It's weird, though, I feel like Nav's habit of spouting facts gives me permission to share my own. In this way he understands me, and in this short time we've been walking he's opened my eyes to a world beyond my sketchpad and paintbrushes. I'm fully awake and still don't want to go home. It's so boring in Reedby. No buskers, no street art, no cafés or bars, just the village pub. I want to go into town with Nav.

"Do you want to go for a drink?" I say quickly and firmly. Nav is startled, as if I've shone a torch into his face. No answer. *Oh no!* He probably thinks I'm trying to chat him up—which I'm not. I just like the idea of hanging out with him. I turn to go.

"Sure," he says. "What about your portfolio? We could drop it at mine."

"You live in the centre of town?"

"No. We are renovating an old shop. It is massive, the size of a warehouse. Technically the place belongs to my uncle. It'll be safe there."

*

The streets become narrower and the shops smaller as we head away from the city centre. At first, Nav carried my portfolio with the ease of someone over six feet tall, now he's stopping more often and changing hands. He doesn't look anything like an art student. His black skinny jeans are too new, and his white T-shirt is too white. He's not the sort of person I usually hang out with, and though it's nice, I notice we are heading towards a part of the city I only go to when I'm visiting Mum at work, at the art school. I realise I don't really know Nav at all.

"Not far now," says Nav, as if noticing my sudden unease.

"A corner shop? Your family's shop?" I ask.

"No. We don't have a *corner* shop," says Nav sharply.

Why did I say that? A racial stereotype from television soaps just fell out of my mouth. Besides, I know from a project we did in Year 10 that most Asian families in Norfolk are working at the hospital or in the hospitality industry. *Is that stereotyping, too?*

"My uncle's office is in what used to be an antiques shop, next door to Gadget Fix," says Nav. "I help out a bit there. That's where I'll mend your phone."

"Can't you mend my phone at home?" I ask.

He looks at me incredulous. *Have I made another faux pas?* "Most phones use tamper-proof screws and glues which can make fixing a phone tricky, but not impossible. Proper tools are important for a better end result. Archie has a whole range of special tweezers, adhesive films…"

"Okay. I believe you!"

"Usually when they have a tricky IT problem and have run out of ideas on how to fix it, they call me," Nav adds, proudly.

Gadget Fix is squashed between a charity shop and a building site.

"Archie and I were at primary school together," says Nav, introducing his mate. "This is Lucie."

33

"Nice to meet you, Lucie," says Archie, standing up. He is only a few inches taller than me, has white-blonde hair and milky coloured skin. The opposite to Nav in almost every way! What they do have in common is the absence of a Norfolk accent. They are both well spoken, which makes them sound posh—just like Mum's cousin Julia's kids, Ollie and Sofia— who went to a private school. Nav and Archie talk tech for a bit whilst I explore the little repair shop.

Gadget Fix is filled with wires and cables and is a bit like walking around the innards of a vast computer. It reminds me of an old film Maisie and I used to watch with Dad. In *Tron* people walked around inside the computer system. The shop is like that, but about a hundred times smaller and messier.

"Leave it with me and come back tomorrow after ten. The big boss is out," says Archie giving Nav a high five. "The workshop out back will be all yours." Archie has a cool hipster beard. *Why is his beard ginger and his hair blonde? Is that all in his DNA?*

We both stand awkwardly on the pavement. "My portfolio, are we taking it to…" I begin.

"We'll drop it next door," interjects Nav.

Next door is a building site. What is he on about?

"My uncle is converting the place into some flats," says Nav pointing to the hoarding, an artist's impression of a futuristic building with a riverside view. "New halls of residence for the art school."

"Yeah, I heard about it. It's going to be like something off *Grand Designs*—all glass, wood and chrome." I say as we walk up to the office entrance.

"I am one of the key holders in case there's a problem with the builders. I'll have to turn the burglar alarm off. So don't panic!" He takes out a key card and pushes on the door. "Strange. It's open. But there's no sign of the builders."

The ground floor of the old shop is a makeshift sales office, which leads into the new build—and the building site. I edge in behind Nav into what I guess will become the reception area. The air is heady with the aroma of spices which smell familiar. The food smell is a complete assault on my senses. Then a secondary smell: plaster, paint and dust. I step past tins of paint, rollers and dust sheets.

Sitting at a glass desk is a man typing into a MacBook. I start and grab Nav's arm. This man, in his late thirties, is dressed to impress in smart jeans and a suit jacket. His black hair is so shiny and neatly coiffed it looks like a wig. On the desk, untouched, is a platter of little silver bowls: curries, fried snacks, yoghurt, rice, breads. Definitely not an intruder!

"Uncle Nabeel!" says Nav.

The man looks up from his laptop. He fixes his stare on me for a moment too long, like he's weighing me up. *Am I being objectified?* Whatever is going on, I don't like it.

"Just leaving this here for a bit. It's heavy," says Nav, propping my portfolio against the wall.

Nav's uncle looks from me to Nav and back to me again.

"You haven't asked why *I* am here?" says Nav's uncle.

"Why are *you* here?" asks Nav as if obliging a truculent toddler. I love the word truculent! We learnt it in English Literature. The benefit of doing an academic A Level alongside Art and Textiles!

"Builders," sighs Nav's uncle.

"Builders? I don't see any builders," says Nav.

"That's the problem. They haven't turned up for several days. We have a deadline. These flats need to be ready for the start of term. I'm going to have to stay on-site, here in Norfolk, until this is sorted. When they finally turn up and see me here, they'll have a surprise. Hands-on management. Just like the old days."

Nav

"We'll be back in a bit for the folder," I say. "Are these going free?" I take a *pakora* from one of the bowls before Uncle Nabeel has a chance to answer. Being busy with Lucie, I haven't thought about lunch.

"Take what you want! A gift from the owner of Tamarind and Spice. You know, the new vegan Indian restaurant up the road? He popped round with this. All a ploy to tell me about his son going to university in Birmingham and needing accommodation."

"Perhaps he was just welcoming you," I want to say. I never know what to make of Uncle Nabeel. He's always so suspicious of people. I guess that's what happens when you're rich, like people who win the lottery and aren't sure who their real friends are anymore. I'm not surprised that Uncle Nabeel doesn't ask me about my A-level results, or my plans to go to university. The same reason I don't tell him how well I've done.

Uncle Nabeel gets up and gives me some paper bags for the food. He whispers in my ear, "Is she *gori*? I can't quite tell. Where is she from?"

For a moment I freeze. I know I should say something rather than let this comment go. I don't like this word used to refer to white people. I know it literally means "white" and isn't derogatory unlike the hideous P-word. But to me it feels divisive. Surely there is more to people than viewing them as these simplified categories. The best I can do to communicate my annoyance is to get out of here quickly. I turn to Lucie. "Let's go!"

Lucie

"Does your uncle stare at everyone he meets in that way?" I ask. I'm also wondering what Nav's uncle said to him that caused his expression to change and prompted our quick exit from the office.

"In what way?"

"Kinda suspicious. Shifty."

"He's a clever businessman. Likes to suss people out," says Nav. "My mum told me that when my grandparents' textile business wasn't doing well back in the 80s and 90s. Uncle Nabeel, who was not long out of school, and probably not much older than I am now, took out a bank loan and bought up a load of properties in Birmingham for next to nothing. He refurbished them. Then gentrification. Yuppies. Student lets. He made his fortune. He made the family a fortune. He's smart, but never went to university. Mum says he's got a chip on his shoulder about educated people who think they know it all."

"A bit like my dad—well step-dad—he didn't go to uni either. He's a builder. He can construct anything!" I say.

"Maybe we should introduce them!" says Nav. "Uncle Nabeel is always on the look out for more workers."

"Dad has too much work! He's booked up for months ahead."

"Want to know something funny about Uncle Nabeel I don't usually tell people." Nav says.

"Yeah, go on!" I push.

"Uncle Nabeel has his own entry on Wikipedia."

"Really?"

"My cousin Karim, who lives in Chicago, posted the listing."

"What does it say?" I ask, half giggling. "I've never met anyone who's listed on Wikipedia."

Nav scrolls down his phone. "It's all in marketing speak. *N S Trading is one of the UK's biggest and brightest property groups, established in 1992 by entrepreneur and current chief executive Nabeel Salman. He holds a portfolio in excess of one billion pounds and is estimated to be worth £145 million. Nabeel Salman is in the top five hundred richest people in the UK and top fifty richest British Asians* blah-blah-blah…"

"Wow!"

We stand on the street corner. "There's a bar, a few minutes away, by the river. The Playhouse. We could go there for that drink?" I say in my most laid-back voice.

"I know it," says Nav, starting to make his way along the street.

"We can take the footpath instead," I say. "The scenic route. I know it well, it's near Mum's office at the art school."

The track is overgrown and it's like entering a secret garden. Butterflies swarm around the buddleia. The purple flowers smell of raspberry jam. Nav waves his arms around against the insects. For a moment I'm disappointed. He reminds me of Cecil Vyse in *A Room with a View*—my favourite GCSE book. The city person, with their head in books, unable to just be with nature.

Nav surprises me and stops to sit at a rickety wooden bench and beckons me to do the same. I almost expected him to take out a clean handkerchief to sit on in the way Mum's friend Cherry does when she comes over for a country walk! I sit down beside him. Side-by-side we stare into the river.

On the far bank a mother scolds her son for throwing stones into the water.

We sit for a long time, absolutely still, watching the hypnotic ripples on the water until Nav opens his backpack and takes out the paper bag of savoury snacks. "Hungry?"

I nod and take one. I bite into the fried parcel. The lightly battered aubergine melts in my mouth. How to describe this heavenly taste? I've heard my parents make pompous comments about wine: delicate, subtle, sweet, tart, elusive. I could say all of this about the *pakora*. It's nothing like the cold, mushed vegetable balls that my mother sometimes buys from the supermarket to take as our family offering to parties.

"These are amazing! As good as my grandma's," says Nav. "Savoury snacks are about the only thing my grandparents' hometown is famous for. I can remember I was only a little kid when we made a trip into the old town of Gojra. I ate so much I was sick on the way home."

"My mum's parents came from Stock in Essex. A dull, Anglo-Saxon sounding place. I don't think Stock is famous for anything! Where's Gojra?" I ask intrigued by the unusual name.

"Gojra's in the Punjab," says Nav.

"That's India, right?"

"The Punjab *is* in the far north of India and *also* part of Pakistan. Gojra is on the Pakistani side of Punjab."

"Oh, how come?"

"The region got sliced in two after partition."

"Partition?"

"Independence from the British, as my father says we should call it. The Great Partition of India was the division of British India which happened in 1947 and created the two independent nations of India and Pakistan. Two of the provinces were divided: Bengal and Punjab. It was based district-wise on Hindu and Muslim majorities. Some of my family went to Pakistan. They believed it was safer for Muslims to migrate to this new country that had been established for Muslim citizens of India. It was one of the world's largest migrations in history. Partition displaced over fifteen million people, and more than a million died."

"That's terrible! How come I don't know this?" I say.

"Dad always says that it should be taught more in schools."

I'm almost angry. The amount of time we spent learning about the Tudor kings and queens, when we could have been learning something that must still affect so many people! Nav's dad is right. "We should all be learning about it as part of the curriculum," I say. "There must be so many important historical events from around the world that I don't know anything about."

"At midnight on the fourteenth of August, India and East and West Pakistan came into existence," continues Nav dramatically. "Nowadays the fourteenth of August is Independence Day in Pakistan and it's the fifteenth of August in India. My dad calls it the vanity of small differences." Nav knows his stuff!

A shiver goes down my spine. "The fourteenth of August is my birthday! I was born just before midnight."

"It's a national holiday in Pakistan. Happy belated birthday for Sunday then," says Nav.

"Thanks."

Nav's face is lost in thought. Is he disappointed in my lack of general knowledge?

"I can tell you that mathematically there should be a 1:365 chance of you having your birthday on the fourteenth of August," says Nav. "That doesn't take into account leap years. Roughly a 1:365.25 chance. But of course, that is obvious."

I stare at him. *Obvious to whom?*

"But this is the thing I was thinking about," he continues. "Birthdays aren't going to be evenly distributed due to social and cultural reasons. I once heard that the rarest day to be born on is December 25, Christmas Day. July 4, American Independence Day, is pretty rare too. I wonder what the data would look like, all mapped out."

I smile. He wasn't judging me at all. I love that. He sees things so differently to me. What's more he doesn't show his knowledge in a bossy way like Mum sometimes does, but in a thoughtful way. It's like clicking on a new tab. The Nav tab. Who wants to have a friend who thinks just like them? I've never heard anyone talk like Nav. I admit it. I was prejudiced. I thought a scientist (a bit of a geeky one too!) couldn't see the world from an interesting perspective in the way that artists often do. But he can. He does. He thinks about things in a creative way—just like an artist! And what a change from some of the pretentious people who were in my art class at college. They thought they were *so* original! Nav's the real deal.

"Tell me more about Pakistan," I say.

"I was a kid the last time we went. There aren't many relatives left there now. Some are in the States, Dubai, and others here in the UK."

"Why did they leave?" I ask.

"Some left for business, as in economic migrants; others for education. Lahore, the capital of Punjab has amazing old buildings…"

I listen to Nav recount stories of intense heat, noise, food, uncles and aunties. "Exactly how many aunties and uncles do you have?" I ask, feeling a little jealous that he's from such a big and interesting family.

"Everyone over a certain age is an aunty or uncle, whether they're related to you or not," he tells me. "It's a respect thing."

Little snapshots of another world. I listen. Well, I am partially listening. Part of my brain is thinking about my own background. That I don't know if I have a big extended family scattered all over the world. I only know fifty per cent of my ancestry. Mum's story. I have *her* story, but I don't have *history*. And that's got me thinking about how the word history is usually about a man's version of the world. I never thought about the word like that before. If only the results were in about the other half of me, I would tell Nav. I just don't know. And I hate not knowing. It makes me feel helpless and insecure—as if it's my fault that I don't know about my *own* family.

"What about you? What about your family?" asks Nav, taking me by surprise. In my limited experience boys usually just like to talk about themselves!

The question I was dreading. *Lucie, change the subject*, I tell myself. "My family isn't very interesting. To be honest I'm more interested in becoming an artist. Look at the river," I say. "You can just think it's any old river, but when you start to look, really look, you notice things. See the light on the water. What colour is it?"

Nav stares at the river as if I've asked the most difficult question in the world. "White-ish?"

"It's not really white. It's yellow, pale mauve, the lightest blue. Then in the shadows there are more colours: indigo, chocolate brown, olive green. It's all about the viewer and their perception."

"You're right," says Nav screwing his eyes up. "I can't believe I never noticed that before."

I wish I had some watercolours. I could paint this view and show him just what I mean about the countless colours and the dancing of the light on water.

"I've sat here before, in the winter, with Archie," he says. "We used to watch ice floes glide down the river—there was something ancient about it; as if it has happened a million times before, which in geological terms it may have done."

An out of time feeling washes over me. "Timeless. The river is the ancient heart of any city," I say dreamily.

Nav goes quiet. Oh no! I think I read that line somewhere. I'm sounding so pretentious.

"Actually, the real reason Archie and I came here was to vape. We didn't think anyone would spot us. One day we tried the apple pie flavour and it made me so sick we never did it or came again!" says Nav.

I laugh. I can't imagine Nav being so reckless. He seems so clear-headed and in control.

"Not surprising really as vape flavourings are chemicals that usually fall into the classes of ketones, aldehydes and alcohols—and not even the sort which makes you drunk! I can't even face normal apple pie these days!"

The play of light and ripples on the water start to give me ideas for a textile design. All of my senses come alive. I wish I had my little pocket sketchbook to draw and write these things down before they slip my mind.

"When I start drawing and developing ideas it's like going into the zone. Being really aware—in the moment. Natalie, my art tutor, calls it flow time when we are all completely immersed in our drawings and paintings. The studio goes quiet and there's an atmosphere of real energy. A kind of active and creative meditation and you never know what the result will look like. It's completely different to say, painting by numbers or those awful mindful colouring books for adults. They are mind*less*."

Nav smiles. He really knows how to listen. His eyes are full of encouragement. And unlike most of my friends, he doesn't switch off or try to change the subject when I start ranting like this. I feel he gets it. He gets me.

"They loved my mind*less* comment at Central Saint Martins. At my degree interview."

"You are an artist already," he says. "You don't need to do a degree."

"Thanks. Do you do anything artistic?" I ask.

"Mum is a mathematician, so when I was a kid her idea of us doing something creative together was to give me graph paper or Islamic pattern colouring books. I guess you'd disapprove of those."

I shrug. "No, I wouldn't. That sounds cool!"

"I think some were even based on the Alhambra palace."

"Like my designs."

"Yeah, but they were more maths than art. 'Finding the shapes and angles in a fun way'," he says in a mocking voice. "They weren't about having your own creative ideas."

I smile and giggle.

"I quite liked the mind*less* colouring. I was on autopilot and let my mind wander. Anyway, what about you? Your family?" he asks, "Your mum is a photographer. Do you think creativity runs in your family?"

"Maybe. Mum used to travel the world taking pictures. If you look up Tori Kitchener, you can see some of her old photos. These days she doesn't even take that many photographs. She teaches part-time round the corner at the art school. My step-dad's a builder, but he can also build any cake you can imagine." It feels disloyal to call Dad my step-dad, but it's accurate isn't it? Dad isn't my biological father.

"Nice. Photography is a mix of art and science. Are you all from around here?"

"My mother's family have lived in East Anglia forever. Essex originally. They're descendants of Viking marauders. Like most people down the east coast." The word Viking is an attempt to match his story. To seem exotic, albeit in a Scandi knitted jumper and cool IKEA design kind of way. He looks at me perplexed. "My mum and sister are fair and have blue eyes." I take another *pakora* and sink my teeth into a lightly battered cauliflower bite. I really want to tell Nav about the DNA test, but I haven't told *anyone*—not even Jenny!

He looks at me. My mouth is full. Time slows down. Is he going to ask about my father's family? I will have to answer: "I don't really know," which is a pathetic answer. A swan and its cygnets glide past.

"Will you survive the evening without your phone?" he asks cheerily, changing the subject.

The moment to tell Nav has passed. "Sure," I say. "Unlike my sister, I'm not addicted to social media. I'll have an evening detox!" Well not completely, I'll have to login on my laptop to see if the results are in.

Nav leans back and picks a fistful of blackberries from the brambles behind the bench. He uncurls his long elegant fingers, "Pudding."

I take a couple.

His phone buzzes. Nav stands up abruptly. He glances at the screen and types a quick message. "Let's go and get that drink," he says.

Nav

The quirky bar is decorated with old theatre props: a battered Beetle car bonnet, a 1950s vintage shop sign and other weird and wonderful things. I leave Lucie to order and go outside. After 5pm you have to bring ID to go into the bar. I might have just got my A-level results and be heading off to university this autumn, but I'm still only seventeen. I skipped a year at school and won't be eighteen for another four months.

There's one table with an empty bench in the garden. "Are these free?" I ask the elderly man who is sitting with a little girl wearing a sequined unicorn T-shirt.

The man smiles and signals for me to sit. I pull the bench out and sit down, leaning back against the fence, overhead are fairy lights and colourful bunting. The whole set-up here is easy-going and pretty, but contrived. I think of my sister Nadiya's Instagram posts and how this scene would fit perfectly into her boho chic aesthetic. My phone buzzes.

> Mum: Where are you? Are you alright?

I can't tell Mum where I am or who I'm with. Underage and in a bar with a girl isn't a conversation I'm prepared to have. Best to say nothing, or as little as possible. How can I text Mum and tell her I want to spend the rest of today with someone I've just met? I know I should be on my way home. I should *be* at home. Dad is picking up fish and chips—my favourite way to celebrate—on his way back from the surgery. Mum promised to escape her maths colleagues in good time, even if it means leaving her team to decide who gets offered a place at their university through clearing. No pressure on me then!

The man and little girl chat away. "Just us two. Nanny's shopping," he says to me. His accent is friendly and reminds me of my relatives who live in the North.

"Norwich is a good place for shopping. The city's got everything, chain stores, one-off independent shops," I say, politely realising I sound like someone at the tourist office. "What's brought you to Norfolk?"

"We're on our holidays!" says the girl excitedly.

"We've got a caravan up at the coast," adds her grandfather. I think of my paternal grandparents, always too busy working to take us out, let alone on holiday.

"Nanny's taken Tommy with her." The girl sips on her straw. "He's soooo annoying."

"Tommy's her little brother," explains the man.

"I've got a younger brother and sister too. They've been sent on holiday to our aunty."

The granddad smiles and says, "So where are you from?"

"Norwich."

"I mean, where are you *originally* from?"

I am so used to everyone asking me this. Here we go. The smile which means so many unsaid things. Nevertheless, I feel my heart pumping. The next question (in so-called polite society) is "What's your heritage?" as if I am like one of the antiques in the bar area. My phone vibrates.

Dad: I'm in the queue at the chip shop. Dad.

Why does he always sign off "Dad"? I know the message is from him!

"You're not from around here?" continues the man.

I reread Dad's message trying to look busy with my phone and finally answer. "I was born in Birmingham. Our family moved here when I was at primary school."

"Thought so. Your accent. You don't say Swaaaafham," he imitates the clichéd Norfolk accent of the market town near Dad's surgery.

"My mum always liked the idea of Norwich, and then she got offered a permanent position at the university here. There aren't many jobs for mathematicians." I add. I smile weakly. What did he really think? Did he see my black hair, dark eyes and brown skin and think that I don't look like I'm from around here? But obviously he wouldn't say that in public. It's *the elephant in room*. In this white, polite city *I* am the elephant in the room.

Lucie places a gin and tonic and a bottle of beer on the table.

"Thanks," I say. I should have told her I don't drink alcohol.

"Is this your sister?" asks the girl.

"No," I say. "My brother and sister are younger. A bit older than you."

She smiles up at Lucie. "You're very pretty. You look like Pocahontas. 'Just around the river bend...'" sings the little girl.

"She was watching the film in the car on the way down. You're a little Disney princess," says the granddad, hastily downing the dregs of his pint. "We have to go and meet Nanny and Tommy."

The girl's face crumples. "I want to stay here all evening."

So do I.

Lucie

Nav and I have the table to ourselves. I can't believe how quickly this afternoon is flying by. The little girl's comment hangs in the air. It isn't the first time someone has said I look like Pocahontas, but it *is* the first time anyone has said I look like I'm related to someone real, rather than on screen! I don't know who I see anymore when I look in the mirror. Let alone who someone else sees.

"At least he didn't think I was a terrorist with this rucksack," says Nav heaving his bag off the ground and back again.

"People think that?"

"Sometimes," says Nav.

"Really? In that case I might be your accomplice." I suddenly realise what a weird thing I've said. I quickly change the subject to college. "My photography lecturer said something about the way I look. You know Martin Harvey?" I continue.

Nav nods. "I've heard his name around college."

"He told me with my tawny skin, green eyes and dark hair it was like looking at 'that girl' in the National Geographic photo. The one from Kashmir, or was it Afghanistan? Whatever. After the tutorial I googled her. And do you know what? She *does* look like me." I pause. "You're the first person I've ever told this to."

Nav looks perplexed. "Why didn't you feel you could tell anyone?"

"Well, it made me feel weird."

"Huh?"

"Nobody else's appearance gets as many comments as mine does. Are teachers even allowed to do that? It felt intrusive.

50

And…it was shocking, freaky, to think that a stranger, from the other side of the world, looked more like me than anyone in my own family."

"You must share some similarities with your mum or sister."

"Mum, Maisie and I have the same lop-sided smile, the same bra size." *Oh no! I've done it again.* He's looking away, embarrassed. "And the same narrow feet," I add hastily.

Too much information! Stop rambling! Is it the alcohol talking? I should have stopped after the second rhubarb gin and tonic—but it tastes so good. Nav didn't touch his pint, so I drank that too. And he is now sensibly drinking lemonade. I watch as he sits awkwardly, there's something about him that just makes me feel at home, it's like I've known Nav my entire life, even though we have different interests. I don't know how else to describe it, but it's like being around someone super close like Maisie, or Jenny. Like we have the same frame of reference for the world.

Nav shrugs disinterestedly. "Everyone, everything is related," he says.

"Maybe," I mutter.

"Yes. Not maybe." Nav replies. "Your DNA isn't so different from a monkey's, or a tomato's. We're all connected."

"That's so Zen. Or is it Shinto?" I say concealing my disappointment at his reductive view of it all. After all it was *me* who told him all about the Mesosphere paintings and how the artist wanted to show how, as humans we are materially connected to everything else, extending to the universe itself. Isn't that a world away from having similar DNA to a tomato or a cucumber? "DNA isn't just about chemical compounds and numbers. What about the individual people, the stories behind the data? Couldn't that be part of scientific research too?" I ask.

"Well, it is and it isn't science," he says. "You'd have to take a DNA test and see what the data says, otherwise it's just observations and conjecture. They're doing a study up at Mum's university on DNA, not about how it impacts looks, but on intelligence."

"Intelligence?" I say. "How would they measure that? For instance, my dad and Maisie can put together a piece of flat-pack furniture before Mum and I have made any sense of the instructions. But Mum and I can write essays and sit exams without it being a big deal. There are so many different types of intelligence."

"That's what my dad says. Although, my mum thinks real intelligence is all about IQ tests."

This is the moment to weave my DNA test into the conversation. The results might even be there waiting for me tonight when I log into my laptop, and I am bursting to talk about it.

Nav's phone buzzes. He drops his gaze and reads the message. His face falls. "Sorry, I have to go, my parents are waiting for me at home."

"What about my portfolio?" I ask indignant.

"Uncle Nabeel will still be there. It's where he hides out. He even has a camp bed in the storeroom, even though there are rumours that the building is haunted. Of course, I don't believe in all that. But he got the old antique shop for a good price and built around it. There was even a stuffed tiger out the back."

"Really? What did they do with it?"

"It went to the local museum, I think."

"Okay, I'll pop back," I say, not letting on that I'm a bit nervous about going back there on my own. There's something disconcerting about the way Nav's uncle stared at me, and now this talk of ghosts is freaking me out!

"Nice to meet you," says Nav politely. He stands up and is gone before I know it. He is like Cinderella fleeing at the stroke of midnight, or the buzz of his phone.

Nav

I walk up the road. My phone buzzes again. I shudder at the thought of how late I am. But to my surprise it's not Dad hassling me. This time it's Mum. She's on my case with a family WhatsApp message.

I much prefer talking to Mum about our shared passion for mathematics than all this family stuff. We're both more comfortable using mathematical language than English or emojis—all of which are poor and awkward substitutes for what we want to say. We once had an amazing discussion about how if everyone communicated in the language of mathematics there would be no divisions, no wars. Misunderstandings around sex, gender, social, economic, politics would disappear. Everyone would all be equal.

I know that I'm a disappointment to her—not that she's actually said it—wanting to use my mathematical prowess to study science. Either way, tonight we will celebrate my achievements over a family meal.

There's a lot of activity on my phone. It's there for everyone to see on **Family Chat**. Mum captions it with "Nav is in the *East Anglian Evening Times*". The picture, a digital code, a range of algorithms, travels through the ether at lightening-speed. It crosses many borders: roads, railways, forests, mountain ranges, seas and oceans to the far reaches of our extended family.

I click on the attachment from Mum and scan-read the article.

East Anglian Evening Times

Local boy achieves some of the highest A-level results in the country. He will take up his place at Peterhouse College, Cambridge to study natural sciences in October. *Among the 300,000 students receiving A-level results this year it is a fair bet that one of this year's top-achieving pupil is Naveed Chowdery from Norwich. A bumper crop of five A* A-levels: biology, chemistry, physics, maths, and computer science. When asked what he'd like to achieve in science, the gifted 17-year-old said, "I've always been interested in genetics. I'd really like to work in that area and make new discoveries."*

Stefan Lasky

I'd like to point out that there are two major inaccuracies here. Not exactly fake news, but nobody calls me Naveed, not even Mr Adams, the vice principal. It's Nav. If you want to know the truth, when I was a kid, there were a lot of Sat Nav jokes—at least no one makes those these days. Sometimes I think my mind is a bit like a Sat Nav with plans and maps in my head—always making connections. Secondly, the journalist hasn't quoted me verbatim. It isn't exactly what I said. I'd mentioned different mathematical models which have yet to be used in the area of genetics. I went to some length to explain this to him.

By the time I finish reading the article my phone is beeping incessantly like an alarm. The article hasn't exactly gone viral, but nevertheless there's a crazy mix of words and inappropriate emojis (a dog, starry night, pound sign...) from Aunty Anooshe in Chicago (as usual I can tell she isn't wearing her glasses), a row of smiley faces from Aunty Mona, and a "Cool" from a second cousin in Karachi who I've never actually met in-person. The beeps and messages continue, like a cascade. I've spent my whole life being discussed by my family as if I'm not there. Which I guess for once is true. I'm technically not in Chicago, Manchester or Karachi. As usual I don't add to their chatter, but appreciate the immediate warmth and celebratory messages. I wonder if I should point out the journalist's inaccuracies. I briefly entertain the idea of sending a message to say I'm taking a gap year just to see the reaction. I chuckle to myself at the horror those two little words would unleash. The truth is, I had wanted to take a gap year. I wanted a year to work, unwind, maybe even travel a little. But a gap year isn't something my high-achieving family would ever see the point of, and so I never broached the subject.

I zoom in on the group photo. There we are: me and my new friend, Lucie Hansen.

Lucie

I push open the door to Nav's uncle's office. My portfolio is slouching against the wall. *Phew!* It's still there. Into the reception area I go. The heady smell of paint, plaster and spice slaps me in the face again. I've always had a heightened sense of smell. As a kid we'd be out for a walk somewhere we hadn't visited before and I'd say, "I can smell water." Mum, Dad and Maisie would look at me if I was mad, then around the corner would be a river or lake. Maybe I could put it to use and create a perfume brand? I could be the next Jo Malone if my art career doesn't work out!

My stomach gurgles noisily. I'm starving. I need something to soak up the alcohol. I scan the space looking for some of the Indian snacks Nav had earlier. There's some on the desk. It wouldn't be stealing, not exactly.

I'm about to make my move when I sense someone else is here. Something kind of ghostly hangs in the air. Maybe I've picked up on a scent, like a sniffer dog. I stop dead. I force my face into a fake, friendly smile. He doesn't smile back. He is there in the shadows by the stairs. Nav's uncle stares right through me and I can't read his expression. I grab my portfolio and rush out the door before he has a chance to speak to me.

Past the cobbled streets and medieval buildings that sell souvenirs to tourists I go. All the while I think about the things I could have told Nav about my family and where I live. It would begin something like this: When I was only six months old my mother, Tori Kitchener, an aspiring photographer, moved us from London to Reedby, a little village in the Norfolk countryside. It was a new start for us. I have no memory of living anywhere else.

It didn't take Mum long to meet Steve and I can't really remember a time before my step-dad, when it was just me and Mum. They married, she became Tori Hansen, and they changed my surname to Hansen too. Mum still uses Kitchener as her professional name for her photography work.

There are still a few people sitting at tables outside the pub near the cinema, otherwise even in the city, it is pretty quiet at night. At least London won't be like that! I take a short cut through an alleyway, past the New Age shop where the windows are crammed with Tarot cards, past the polished flint wall. If I was with Dad he'd stand and admire it for a bit, saying, "Isn't it beautiful? The largest flint wall in Norfolk." I touch the wall, the shiny black flints which have been here for hundreds of years, and walk on.

What would I tell Nav about my dad? Steve Hansen is blonde and blue-eyed, and a couple of years Mum's junior. Originally, he came from Thorpe Market, a little village up on the north Norfolk coast, Steve's certain he's descended from Viking marauders. "Is that something to be proud of?" a friend of my parents once asked whilst we were finishing off Dad's amazing pesto lasagne. The drunken dinner party conversation grew heated. Dad shrugged and began to clear the table. One of them added, "There's probably some truth in the Viking connection, as Thorpe is from the Old Norse, meaning farmstead." *I wonder if I have any Viking DNA?*

Then there's my kid sister, Maisie. Physically she's Dad's female doppelganger. She is a pale, blue-eyed blonde; whereas my skin is caramel brown and I have dark green eyes. No one ever thinks we are related, yet alone sisters.

Once when I was seven or eight, we all went to the park on the edge of the village by the allotments. It was autumn and the trees were glowing orange and there were giant sunflowers along the footpath which towered over me and Maisie.

Mum sat at the rickety picnic table chatting to some old woman from the village. We were on the swings and Dad was doling out even-handed pushes and Maisie and I were screaming, "Higher! Higher!" We soared higher and higher rippling through the air.

Suddenly Mum was there beside the swings. "We're off!" she said.

"Don't be a kill-joy," said Dad, nevertheless slowing down the swings.

"Do you know what that woman said to me?" asked Mum.

"What did she say that was such a problem?" he asked.

Mum looked at me and away again. "The woman said: you're so good adopting that little girl. Is she from Romania? One of those poor orphans?"

"What on earth was she thinking?" said Dad.

"I told her calmly, 'She's my daughter.'"

"Our daughter," added Dad taking my hand as I jumped off the swing.

They thought I was too young to understand what was going on. But it was then I knew for sure that I wasn't like the rest of the family.

I head round to the bus station for the last bus to Reedby. I'd tell Nav that this time of year the village isn't too bad a place to live. The riverside pub tables fill up with holiday makers. Cruisers are moored where the chain ferry once ran. Our family has its ups and downs like anyone else. Maisie, always one for the spotlight, has been hard work at times, always wanting everyone's attention. Even nowadays Mum is sometimes called into school about her. Always the same old question. How best to support Maisie?

Me, on the other hand, I just get on with things. They say I am the easier, the quieter daughter. But when the results of my DNA test arrive that will all change.

The City Hall clock strikes seven o' clock. I need to get a move on. The bus station is in view, and I run dragging my portfolio on the pavement. In the distance Ann, our elderly neighbour boards the bus. She sits down at the front near the driver. She watches me run. I wave. She waves back. *Isn't she going to tell the driver to wait?* After all, this is the last bus home. And I don't have my phone to call Mum or Dad to come and get me if I miss it!

The engine revs up. I wedge my portfolio into the miniscule gap between the closing doors, forcing Martin, the driver, to let me aboard. Ann and the rest of the passengers watch me as if I'm acting out a scene from their favourite TV soap. In fact, one girl around twelve years old and sitting on the back seat looks like she is filming the whole thing. *Since when has my life been so interesting?*

I fumble for my ticket. "Don't worry. Just go and sit down," says Martin. I look around the packed bus. There is only one free seat, next to Ann. I turn to smile at my next-door neighbour, forcing the woman to move her shopping down into the foot well and let me and my portfolio sit down beside her.

Even though I've known Ann for years, if I'm being honest, she is a little odd. Ann makes conversation through the fumy stops and starts of the city traffic. Finally, we are out onto the open road. "Where's Maisie?" she asks. She's always preferred Maisie to me. Once she turned up at our door with Easter eggs for us both. Maisie got an enormous egg in shiny pink packaging and I, on the other hand, was given a chocolate buttons egg in a tiny purple box. What a shame she isn't with me now to jolly Ann along. Maisie always seems genuinely interested when Ann talks about the weather, or holidaying in the Isle of Wight or the vagaries of the parish council.

"I'm lucky to have such good neighbours," says Ann. It takes a moment for the penny to drop and realise she is talking about my family. "Steve was there in two minutes when the bath tap wouldn't turn off. He didn't even bat an eyelid at the sight of me wrapped in a small bath towel banging on your front door. I was so scared. You don't know what it's like living all alone."

Sometimes I think I'd love to have our house all to myself. Living alone would be such a luxury. I could get up and go to bed whenever I wanted. I could eat whenever I wanted. I could invite people over whenever I wanted. But instead of saying any of this I nod in agreement.

"Your dad tells me you're off to art college," says Ann.

"I got all the right grades today."

"Well done! You were always a clever little girl. Where are you going to study? Where your mum works?"

"No, London."

"Your mum and dad must be a bit worried, all alone in the big city. In my day my parents worried about IRA bombings when I went on a day trip to London." Ann puts her hand to her mouth. "I shouldn't have said that. Don't want to put you off, these days you can get knocked over crossing the road," she laughs. "But you mustn't worry. That'll be nice for you to be in the city. You'll be with more people like you."

I'm not going to reply to that. I'm not sure if I want to know what she means by "people like you". We sit in silence and I can't wait to get home.

*

The bus pulls up outside Ann's little bungalow as if her garden gnomes are an official bus stop. "Cheerio," she says.

"Bye, Ann," I reply.

That woman is crazy! "People like you." What did she mean by that? I suppose she could mean being in London alongside artists and designers? But it feels more likely that she was alluding to the fact that I don't look like I fit in here, in the village I've always called home?

My head aflame with fury, I navigate my portfolio down the bus steps, wishing I could have said something back to Ann about the "people like you" comment, but as per usual it's impossible to think of the right response in the heat of the moment.

Mum is standing by the open front-door pretending not to be watching out for the last bus. I'm not eleven and on my first bus trip into town! Then I remember my phone. The lack of it.

"How did you get on?" Mum asks unable to restrain herself.

"Got my grades," I say.

"Well done! When we didn't hear, I thought all sorts."

"Sorry, Mum."

"What happened?"

"My phone broke," I explain. "I should have used someone else's and called. Sorry." I could have used Nav's. I don't say that. Welling up inside me is my encounter with Nav. All through the bus journey home whilst Ann rambled on, Nav was on my mind. I've never met anyone quite like him before. It felt really liberating being with someone who looked a little like me, and importantly he had so many interesting thoughts and ideas. I'm usually polite and chat to Ann and the other neighbours. Mum and Dad always say, "It's such a small village you have to avoid making enemies." But today I couldn't be the nice girl-next-door smiling politely at Ann's barbed comments. Then there's the encounter with Nav's uncle which creeped me out. His whole demeanour was just weird.

We go into the dining room and the table is already set for four. In the centre are a plate of poppadoms and a bottle of prosecco. A re-run of my birthday dinner! "Dad's slaving away in the kitchen making your favourite: chicken jalfrezi and chips."

"Ah! That's so sweet."

"Out of a jar, but there's fresh coriander for garnish," adds Mum shrouding the bottle in a tea towel desperately trying to unscrew the cork.

"I'll do that," says Dad coming into the dining room flouting his apron: a printed image of a bra and suspenders—a Christmas present from Nana Pat! He looks at me expectantly, his blue eyes asking, *How did you get on?* all the while performing his manly duty of opening the bottle of fizz. *Bang!* Dad pours a little of the sparkling wine into each of the four glasses and does the rounds again.

"I got my grades. All As and an A* for Art," I say.

Dad puts the bottle down and gives me a bear hug. He steps back and passes me a glass of bubbly. "Cheers!" He announces. We clink glasses. I take a tiny sip. Sometimes, especially during moments like this, I wish that Steve was my real, biological father. Then we'd be a perfect, normal family and I wouldn't need to even think about a DNA test.

"Are you alright?" he asks giving me a look which says, *I know what you've been up to.* Or am I imagining that he's looking at me oddly? Do I look like I've been out drinking? Do I look like someone who is waiting for the results of a DNA test?

"I'm a bit queasy. It's so fumy on the bus and Martin was speeding round the bends," I say side-stepping the question.

"Can't blame him wanting to finish his shift and get home," says Mum.

Mum hardly ever travels by bus. How would she know? It's another world!

"Maisie! Dinner!" she calls.

The four of us take our regular seats round the table. Mum always faces the framed photograph of a market stall. The one she took when she was on her travels around India: the sacks and bowls of gold, orange and red spices resemble an abstract fabric design. Dad faces the kitchen so he can keep an eye on things. Maisie and I both get a garden view. It's like at school, people always sitting in the same seat. Will someone sit in my place when I go to university?

"So, you're back," says Maisie stating the obvious and taking a poppadom before passing the plate to me. "What did you get?"

I tell her my grades quickly so as to not show off.

"Cool," says Maisie.

Mum attempts to refill our glasses. I put my hand out. "That queasy after the bus?"

I nod and pour myself a glass of water. "The smell of the diesel was disgusting."

"They should have electric buses," says Maisie. "We should lobby the bus company!"

Mum begins to recount the various embarrassing situations when I've been car sick. Maisie and Dad laugh. I might have got three As for A-level and an A* for Art & Design, rather than Maisie's predicted batch of borderline passes for GCSE, but I'm still the butt of the family jokes.

I endure the meal. Mum, Dad and Maisie have all these ideas about putting the world to right. Which is fair enough. But they never actually *do* anything. I won't be here soon using this rubbish public transport where you can only pay in cash. I'll be taking the Tube and London buses.

I can't wait any longer to go to my room and turn my laptop on. "I need to message Jenny and let her know my results," I say edging out of the dining room. I wonder if she's got hers. Not that she needs them with her unconditional offer. I also want to look up Nav, I'm intrigued about his family and want to play detective, maybe I'll check his social media and connect on there. Of course, I don't tell Mum that.

Mum clumsily pours the remaining prosecco into her glass. It bubbles over the flute. Dad clears away the dishes. Maisie has already collapsed onto the sofa and is plugged into her phone. No one minds or notices my quick exit. I thought this was supposed to be an evening celebrating my A-level results. I don't care. My other results must be in, and I can't wait to find out.

I wish Jenny was here, chatting and lounging on my bed. I wouldn't feel half as nervous with her around. I switch on my laptop. Do I tell her about Nav? How do I write anything about meeting this interesting guy who really "thinks outside the box"? We're like opposite sides of the same coin. I've always hung out with art students, but an afternoon with science-buff Nav had been so much fun, so chilled.

Jenny may be my best friend, but she isn't always the world's best at keeping a secret, so I don't want to say anything about the DNA test until I know the result. Otherwise, by the time she reaches somewhere with signal she may have told

65

our whole friendship group, and I might still be waiting for the result! I write the briefest of messages.

Lucie: Got my grades. Going to Central Saint Martins!

I check my emails. A notification pops up saying my DNA results are in. I click on the link. DNA Ancestor Heritage fills the screen. My heart is pounding. Scared. Excited. The point of no return. It occurs to me that I don't really know or understand what DNA actually is. If Nav were here I could ask for a proper explanation. None of that we share loads of similar DNA with tomatoes stuff! I want to know about human DNA. I click on a new tab and search DNA. I add "simple explanation" to the search. A bossy voice enters my head and says, "Lucie, are you putting off opening your results?" *Maybe! Definitely!*

I gaze at the DNA definition tab. Part of me wishes I hadn't looked it up. It is so hard to get my head around:

DNA stands for Deoxyribonucleic Acid. DNA is an amazing substance that contains the genetic code DNA is an amazing substance that contains the genetic code: the instruction manual and factory floor for making living things. Each molecule of DNA is enormous in comparison to molecules of oxygen and water. It is made of billions of atoms that, in humans, can form molecules about 5cm long.

A DNA molecule is shaped like a twisted ladder: a double helix (double spiral). It is made of atoms of carbon, oxygen, hydrogen, nitrogen and phosphorus—nothing else. The "rungs" of the ladder hold the long "legs" of the ladder together. In certain conditions, the rungs break in the middle and the legs of the ladder unzip.

This is too much information to take in for someone who stopped thinking about such things after GCSE Double Science. But I need to make up for my lack of scientific knowledge, so I power through and read on.

> *Each half-helix separates, and then re-combines with the other atoms it needs to replicate the original structure. The two separate legs make the other legs they need from surrounding bits and pieces until there are two ladders. This process repeats because DNA has self-replicating molecules.*
>
> *A human female egg cell contains only half the DNA needed to make a baby. It is coiled up and protected by proteins in 23 packages called chromosomes. The other half comes from the 23 other chromosomes brought in by a sperm cell.*

The phrase: *The other half comes from the 23 other chromosomes brought in by a sperm cell* freaks me out. It is as if it knows what I was thinking earlier about *her*story and *his*tory!

> *The chromosomes all work together to create a cell that divides and divides and eventually specialises, to make bone cells, muscle cells, brain cells, blood cells and everything else that makes up the human body.*

I take a deep breath and return to DNA Ancestor Heritage. I stare into the screen. For someone who remembered so many quotes for their English literature exam, I could never remember which password I've used for which account. That's how Frida Kahlo became my password for everything. How many other people have Frida Kahlo as their password? I smile inwardly. Frida was such a fearless woman. I need to be brave too and open my results. Here goes!

Incorrect password shouts back at me. I sign in again, trying to remember which characters are capitals, and which are lower case. Does it want numbers too? I add 14—my birthday. And again, *incorrect password* yells back. I hunt around for password reset. Nothing. Will I be logged out forever if I get it wrong for the third time? Why didn't I leave the sign-in open, like I did on my phone? Think, Lucie, think. I type FridaKahlo%14—no spaces. *Success!* A new page begins to load.

Two-step authentication is enabled. Please enter the one-time password that has been sent to your mobile device. The words flash up on the screen filling me with a sense of doom.

Your mobile device. I'm flooded with indignant rage. No way! How can they do this? It's *my* account! *My* DNA. But there's no way around this.

I'm well and truly locked out.

Friday 19th August

Lucie

I tip cornflakes into my favourite bowl: the one with yellow and red diamond patterns. I pick up the milk carton and pour.

"You're spilling it!" yells Maisie.

The milk pools on the wooden table. I must've zoned out for a moment.

"What's up?" asks Maisie.

"Nothing's up," I lie, laying sheets of kitchen roll on the milky puddles.

She looks at me, in that weird, knowing way she's always done. People take Maisie for an airhead, but she always knows when I'm upset and trying not to show it. "I saw the photo. The one of you in the newspaper." Maisie taps into her phone and flashes the image under my nose.

"It's by that photographer whose picture of the homeless woman begging in the street went viral. The one with the Horus tattoo."

"He's cool. You're famous by association. Is that why you're in a funny mood?"

"No! I'm not in a mood," I snap.

"The beggar photo got thousands of likes on Instagram!"

"Whose Instagram?" says Mum entering the kitchen. Mum's trying Instagram as a platform to share her photos. She'd be over the moon if she got hundreds, let alone thousands of likes!

"Doesn't matter. But look at this photo of Lucie and the other nerds holding up their amazing A-level results in the newspaper," says Maisie waving her phone around.

Mum turns to me. "You didn't tell us you were in the paper. Always a dark horse," says Mum, smiling proudly.

For sure I didn't tell anyone. I thought Maisie would call me a nerd which, to prove the point, she's just gone and done! But the main reason is that I'm too embarrassed, too self-conscious to show Mum a picture which includes Nav. She's bound to ask who the others are in the photo. I think my reticence is all because he looks sort of like me, and in a crazy way this feels disloyal to Mum, especially now that I'm waiting for my DNA results.

I take my bowl to the sink and whisper to Maisie, "White unicorn." Our secret code: white unicorn means escape the parents and hide out in the treehouse. We invented it when we were kids after reading the *My Secret Unicorn* books. It now sounds a really childish thing to say, but we both know what it means.

"Isn't anyone going to show me the picture?" says Mum.

"It's on the *Anglian Evening Times* online site. Or you can buy the paper," I say making my escape.

From the treehouse we survey our kingdom: the neighbours' gardens, hedges, fences and fields. Next door, Ann is in the greenhouse, wearing her tartan gardening pyjamas and picking cherry tomatoes.

Maisie holds out her phone and films a panorama of the chocolate brown and golden stubble fields and posts it to her stories on Instagram. So much for having a secret meeting!

We lie down, bare legs up against the low wooden walls and heads resting on tatty red cushions which used to be on the sofa when we were little. For a moment I wish Jenny was here, rather than my younger sister. I can really talk to Jenny. Or better still, Nav. There's something liberating about talking to him, maybe it's because he hasn't known me forever so he just takes me at face value.

Before Maisie was on social media this was always the place of secrets. She told me about her crush on Mr. Daubier, the French teacher and how much money she had in her running away fund. I'd suggested running away to the south of France, which looking back was extremely reckless advice! Occasionally I shared a secret or two. The usual format is that Maisie is bursting with confessions, and I pretend to be some kind of psychotherapist.

Today I know what it's like to be the one about to explode: the need to tell, to offload. The problem is I don't know quite how to say it. Words are utterly useless sometimes. Maybe I should draw how I feel? I would look like one of Picasso's cubist portraits. My body would be fragmented and made of disjointed angles and sharp planes.

"If you could choose between being able to fly or wearing an invisibility cloak, what would you choose?" asks Maisie.

"What?"

"To fly or be invisible? Which power?"

Maisie is always obsessed with these types of questions and usually as the sensible older sister I humour her. "Today, I would fly."

"Why?" shouts Maisie, excitedly.

"So, I could fly faraway from here," I reply.

Ann turns and looks up before heading off to refill her watering can.

"You know why she's always out there?" Maisie asks, tipping her chin in Ann's direction.

"Gardening," I say matter-of-factly.

"Honestly Lucie! For someone so clever—all those As—you can be really dumb. Ann's got the hots for Dad," cries Maisie. "Remember when she came round wearing that skimpy towel? You could see her boobs trying to burst out! She was all eyes for Dad."

"That's gross! She must be about twenty years older than Dad!"

"He said it was a plumbing emergency, but maybe it was all part of her plan to lure him into her house," laughs Maisie.

"It *was* a real emergency. She was in a right panic. There was water leaking everywhere. Dad was in a state of shock. I've never seen him that worried," I say, suddenly realising that was the same way Nav's uncle looked at me when I turned up in the shop. The intense look on his face was shock. Why was he so unnerved by my presence?

Maisie gives me a hard stare.

"What?" Have I spoken my innermost thoughts out loud? Change the subject away from yourself! This usually works. "Ann looks like Dad, don't you think?"

"Trust you to notice that, forever the artist," says Maisie screwing her eyes up and looking at Ann bent over by the water butt. "You're right."

"Same oval face, large forehead and straw-coloured hair. Maybe they're related?" I suggest.

"She could be his aunt or long-lost sister," says Maisie. "Like on that TV show, my long lost relative, or whatever it's called." Maisie pauses. "On the romantic front though, I thought that opposites attract. Magnetism."

"Really? Are you sure?"

"Example number one: The Fords. They're totally different," says Maisie.

"Who?" I ask.

"You know. Mum and Dad's friends. The beady-eyed history teacher and his right-on wife. She's dark haired, dark eyed and he's mousy and freckled. And they're always all over each other. Disgusting!"

"Yuck! But she *is* beady-eyed too. And they both have beaks for noses!"

We laugh loudly. Maisie types into her phone.

"What are you doing?" I ask.

"I'm checking this out." She taps into her phone and scrolls down the screen. "Ah! *Opposites do attract*. This one says: *Opposites don't attract*. There are loads of articles titled: *Why men and women choose partners who look like their parents...* And Mum does look a bit like Nana Pat. There's also this article: *Why we choose to hang out with friends who look like us.*"

"Maisie, these articles all conflict with each other!" Maisie never had the best analytical mind. She shrugs, and puts her phone down, looking at me expectantly. I'm not so sure now if I want to tell her anything. I'm so frustrated with myself for getting locked out of my DNA Ancestor Heritage account, and now the anticipation is stressing me out. I need to see my DNA results soon. I need to know who I really am. I open my mouth to make an excuse to leave the treehouse, when we hear Mum shouting out for me in the garden. I pop my head out of the treehouse entrance.

"There's someone on the phone for you." Mum shouts up.

"The landline? Who?" I ask.

She shrugs. I slowly make my way down and into the house. Only Nana Pat and people trying to sell us something call the landline. Then I remember. Of course! It must be Nav calling about my phone. I rush into the house.

Nav

The house is deadly quiet without Muni and Nadiya. I never thought I'd miss my younger brother and sister. Mum is at work. It's just me and Dad. I head back to my bedroom leaving Dad to loiter around. He's mooching from one room to the next checking it's clean and tidy. *When are you going to work? I want to ask. Please don't be on a late shift!* That will mean him hanging around all morning. Unless it's even worse, and he's taken the day off to get ready for Aunty Mona's arrival and Muni and Nadiya's return. My parents never tell me their plans and yet they expect to know the exact details of my comings and goings.

I should call Lucie. But I need the house to myself to do it properly, otherwise there's always the possibility of being interrupted. I'm not used to chatting to girls, or having girls as friends. Before sixth-form Archie and I were at an all-boys' school, and even at sixth form college there were just five girls in my physics class, and I sat with the boys in maths and chemistry.

I could go out and walk down the road, or even round the garden but it doesn't change the fact that the thought of speaking, rather than being able to send a message, makes my heart pound. I gather my thoughts, like at the start of an exam. I rehearse my lines. What will I say if her parents answer? "I'm a friend from college. Nav. With news about the broken phone." That doesn't sound too weird, does it? My worst nightmare would be working in a call centre where you have to read out a script to an angry person on the other end of the line.

I'll have her phone fixed later this morning, once I get down to *Gadget Fix*. I should wait until it's mended before calling her. But I just need to know that she will be there to collect it. I really do hate making phone calls, but it's now or never. *Do it now!* I tell myself. My hand shakes as I type in her number.

"Nav. You'll have to get a pizza out of the freezer for lunch. Mum's doing a shop on the way home," says Dad crashing into my room without knocking.

I hit end call. "Sure."

"What are you going to do with yourself today?" asks Dad.

"I'll start on my reading list for Cambridge," I lie. I can't tell Dad that I'm going to help Archie at *Gadget Fix* Repair. Dad will just give me some money and tell me to get on with my studies. I certainly can't tell him I'm going into town to fix a friend's phone.

"Are you alright?" asks Dad.

I nod.

"You can't be serious about starting to study today. Take it easy. Term doesn't begin until October. It's important to have a break," says Dad slowly dragging out each word, staring into me, as if I'm one of his patients.

"Okay," I say.

Finally, the front door slams. Dad's Range Rover crunches over the gravel and out of the drive. *Don't get distracted*, I tell myself. *Just press the button and call Lucie.* The phone rings and rings. Finally, someone answers. She's really friendly and says she'll go and fetch Lucie from the garden.

Lucie

I catch a lift with Mum into town. I tell her I'm meeting up with Sam and Josephine from my old English Literature class. The lie slips out of my mouth before I know it.

"Text me if you want a lift back. Oh, but you can't without your phone," says Mum clicking on the car lock. "You can always come and find me in my office. I won't be staying late, though; I've got my book club tonight."

"I can get the bus," I snap, nervous at the proximity of the art school car park to the gadget shop.

Mum stands motionless by the car. "Do you want me to give you some cash to get a new phone?"

This is unlike Mum. She never offers cash handouts. "I like my old one," I say.

"It's not like you to be so attached to a device. Maisie would have taken the cash and run."

We both smile. Maisie's track record with money is appalling. Even now, she spends all her school dinner money on Mondays and Tuesdays and by Wednesday pesters Mum and Dad to top up her account.

Part of me wishes I could tell Mum the real reason that *only* my old phone will do. I'm pretty certain that only my old phone will give me access to the results, the answer to the question of my ethnicity: Where are you *really* from? I always tell people I was born in London and then we moved to Norfolk when I was a baby. They're never satisfied with that. Always pushing on, asking, "Yes, but where are you really from originally?" As if my answers are never good enough. I am never good enough.

I drift off into a daydream about all this.

"Is your mum Spanish, or maybe Greek?" They often ask.

"No. My mum's famous person double is Ophelia."

"Ophelia?" they ask.

I divert the conversation to an explanation of the pre-Raphaelite painting of Ophelia. I show them an image on my phone. She is floating in water, holding a rose and surrounded by greenery. Lizzie Sidall, an artist in her own right, modelled for Millais in a bath! No pain, no gain to recreate Shakespeare's singing beauty before she drowns in a river. I tell them it's the most visited painting in the Tate. My mother is an icon of English beauty.

Occasionally I recount the sperm donor story. Their faces soften, followed by a bewildered and embarrassed look. They must wonder why she didn't choose a father who looked more like her, created a fatherless daughter who was a clone of herself. Or is my mother a radical, some kind of feminist champion of multiculturalism?

The worst times are when we travel *en famille*, as Mum calls our family group using her best French regardless of where we're travelling to! Checking in at a hotel in France or Italy they'd take our passports and always loiter over mine. Frowning, they would ask, "Where are you from?" Mum and Dad would get twitchy, and the unspoken rule was to say the UK. They never elaborated further. The awkward check-ins thus erased from our holiday story.

"You haven't brought a jacket," says Mum, pulling into the car park and interrupting my train of thought.

"It's August! I'm good."

Mum goes round to the boot of the car and picks up her silver strong box of photography equipment.

Outside, my bare arms disagree. I have goosebumps, unaccustomed to the chill in the air. This morning has the feel of a new term about to begin.

"See you later, then," says Mum. She walks down the riverside path, pausing to look at the light flickering across the water and the misty sky. Is she going to take a photograph before heading to work? Sometimes, in the first year of college, I used to go into her work and meet her for a lift home. I often sat and did my homework there. It's such a stylish space—all *Grand Designs*—medieval stone and modern glass.

I hang around a bit browsing the charity shops before continuing down the road, past Nav's uncle's own *Grand*

Designs development. Through the window I can see a couple of strip lights are on.

I walk on in the direction of Gadget Fix. My step and my heart lighten. I know I'm early but maybe he will have fixed my phone already.

Nav

Each time the shop door opens it could be her. But rather than hoping with each door ring that it's Lucie, I'm dreading it. I'm not sure how to tell her what's happened. Is this how Dad feels when he has to give a patient a difficult diagnosis? I know a malfunctioning phone isn't a life or death situation. Yet it feels like it right now. Why did I have to tell her that I could fix it? I was going to replace the cracked screen, with a shiny new one. But it was pointless. When I finally managed to turn the phone on, it was glitching badly and it's a miracle I've saved so much of her information. The last of the photos are safely transferring onto the laptop.

Of course, I haven't looked at the photos, though it's always tempting. Dan who used to work here was fixing some guy's phone once and found the funniest photos on there of an obviously raucous bachelor party. He found it hilarious, though he quickly stopped laughing when management found out and he got sacked. I also know all about confidentiality and data protection from my father so there no chance of crossing that line. Plus, I'd like to think Lucie and I are friends. Nevertheless, a photo of her artwork might make the perfect screensaver. I've never been friends with an artist before. I've had my current screensaver, of the periodic table, for over a year. I've known the elements off by heart for years so you'd think there's not much point having it. Except that it gives me a feeling of limitless possibilities. Like the way you can gaze at a map for ages and let your mind wander. Would a screensaver of Lucie's designs do the same?

"Archie!" I yell.

He crashes into the workshop. For someone who can perform intricate surgical operations on the smallest pieces of tech, Archie normally blunders around like someone with no coordination at all. At school everyone made fun of his clumsiness. Whereas, for some reason I can't explain, I kind of like that about him.

"I've moved the photos and got the sim card out. Have you got a similar phone to this?" I ask, showing him the model.

"I can do you a deal on the latest version."

"What sort of deal?" I ask. That's another thing about Archie, since he went on his apprenticeship; he's become a savvy businessman. An entrepreneur who seizes any opportunity just like my Uncle Nav! I know that's why he's out the front and I'm in the workshop. I'm interested in tech. I'm not a deal maker.

"Come and help me this Saturday and it's yours for free."

"Sure. Cool."

Archie throws a box onto the work bench and I set about preparing Lucie's new phone. She's going to be so pleased.

Ding. The shop bell. We peer round into the shop. "Is that her?" whispers Archie.

"Yes," I say pulling myself together and going into the shop.

It's all going to be okay, I tell myself. Although part of me stills feel bad about accidentally breaking her phone. "Hi," I wish I could say more than hi. I wish I had Archie's sales patter. I physically can't open my mouth to say anything more. There may not be any scientific rationale to this but I am speechless! And in the long moment of wondering how I will break both the good and the bad news about her phone situation, I notice that I was incorrect in thinking her hair was the same colour as mine. Her hair is dark brown, but in this light there are copper highlights. It's glowing. Is there some kind of electro-chemical process, fluorescence, or even phosphorescence going on? Her green eyes are glowing. She's smiling. I'll start with the good news. I can't wait to tell her I've got her the latest model. A brand-new phone for free!

Lucie

Nav is standing in the shadows by the doorway to the workshop. The artist in me is taking in all the details of his face. If I was to paint his portrait, I'd use rich earthy colours: raw umber, burnt Sienna. I glance at my hands on the shop counter. My fingers are a lighter hue of brown. In layman's terms we'd be on the same DIY paint colour card—with me a few bands lighter. So unlike Mum, Dad and Maisie who are on a different paint card altogether! Am I obsessing about skin colour? It's just that around here nearly everyone is on Mum, Dad and Maisie's paint card. Sometimes this makes me feel special; other times it makes me feel as if I don't quite belong.

Nav holds up a new phone. "So, this is the good news," he proudly explains how this is now mine. He starts telling me all about how much better this one is than my old phone. He's all excited about processing speed and camera specifications, but the information all washes over me.

My phone. I need *my* phone.

"What's the bad news?" I say slowly.

Nav wrinkles up his face. "Your old phone glitched and died. I couldn't save it," he says, as if emerging from an operating theatre.

All my hopes are dashed. This phone doesn't have the *one* thing I really need—access to my DNA Ancestry account. How am I supposed to access my results?

"Were you lying to me when you said you could fix it?"

"No. Of course not! But this is a much better model," explains Nav nervously as if everything is okay. Which it is not.

"I want my old phone to work. I don't want this new one."

"This is crazy!" says Archie, moving to stand beside Nav and looking at me as if I'm a spoilt brat. "Most customers would be more than happy. Especially when this is all for free!"

Nav is silent. He looks down at the counter.

How can I tell them I'm mad at myself, not them, for being too paranoid. For setting up crazy security measures and getting locked out of my DNA test account? I need a miracle or a super hacker. I'll never find out my results. I look ungrateful, I know, so I'm embarrassed on top of being upset.

"Thank you," I say as brightly as I can manage, taking the phone and rushing out of the shop.

I march down the road as if I'm in a hurry to get somewhere. I have no particular destination in mind. I'm slowed down by the pedestrian crossing. Mums with buggies block the pavement. Do I take a chance and step into the road with the on-coming traffic? My sensible self kicks in, so I channel my frustration by pressing the button over and over again.

"It won't change any quicker, love," says a woman at the start line with her shopping trolley ready to race the buggies.

She's right. The green man doesn't appear any faster. It's then I feel a presence behind me; someone standing too close. I turn. "Are you following me?"

"No," says Nav.

"You just happened to be right behind me?"

"I need to cross the road. It's a public place."

The red man refuses to turn to green. I feel stuck in so many ways. I was meant to get answers, but I just got in my own way. Nav broke my phone and promised to get it fixed, but I guess that didn't work out either. I can feel tears well up in my eyes.

"Okay well, thanks for your help with the phone."

I say to myself: *on your marks, get set...* and ready to go, ready to make a quick getaway.

"I put all your photos on the new phone. I didn't look at them, if that's what you're thinking."

I shrug. A lump forms in my throat.

Nav does the silent act again all the while looking at me with a slight frown. No. It's more than that. He looks disappointed. Sad. "What's really up?" he asks.

"Nothing's *really* up!" I lie. The lights change and I'm off.

Nav

Keeping my distance, I follow Lucie. I bend down and pretend to tie up my trainers. I've watched this kind of surveillance procedure in the movies. I stand back up and there she is. Lucie has doubled-back and is right in front of me. Her face is millimetres from mine. *Please don't shout or scream! Not in public!*

"Do your mathematical skills extend to code breaking?" she asks.

This is the last thing I expect her to say. "What like GCHQ, Bletchley Park and all that?" I ask. "We went on a Computer Science trip to Bletchley Park. It's amazing." I start telling her all about the breaking of the Enigma code during World War Two.

Lucie smiles for the first time since leaving the shop, though her eyes look blurry like she may have been crying.

Maybe she'd like to do a day trip to GCHQ? The house looks like a stately home and has a café and everything. It's free to go in, and more interesting than most places where people hang out; better than a cinema or bowling alley any day! I'm wondering how to suggest this when she whispers, "Can you hack?"

"Of course, I can hack," I say. Immediately I'm taken back to when I was thirteen years old. "I nearly got expelled from school for hacking."

"What did you do?"

This all sounds very childish now, but nevertheless I confide in Lucie. "Archie and I programmed the school computer screens so they displayed luminous green type falling down the monitor like in *The Matrix*."

She smiles again. "That sounds cool. How did you get found out?"

"The IT technician."

"What else have you hacked?" she asks excitedly.

"You don't want to know," I say enigmatically.

"Go on, tell me!" she nudges.

"The school librarian had a thing about Paul Hollywood from *The Great British Bake Off…*"

Lucie nods. "Maisie and I always watch it with Dad when Mum is out with her friends."

"…so we hacked her computer. The printer in the library wouldn't stop churning out mugshots of Paul Hollywood!"

"Really!" she says grinning. "Were you in big trouble for that?"

"I think we got off lightly. We only had to do one day of isolation even though we initially denied it and they had to bring in the ICT teacher to work out who was responsible!"

She laughs. "Oh you're a pro!" Then she says, "Sorry about earlier, I was out of order. Do you want to grab a coffee?"

I shrug. "Yeah sure!" We continue down the road. I've never known what people meant when they said they're so happy it's like "walking on air" (technically we already walk through air), but I think this is it! Right now, the world is on my side. To tell the truth, it's been ages since I've made a new friend. People usually dismiss me as boring and nerdy. If this is what it will be like when I get to university and hang out with new and interesting people, I'm feeling much more positive about going to Cambridge.

Every other building is a café. Why do people need so many coffee shops? I've never noticed it before. Caffeine is the opiate of the masses. Lucie heads into a tiny café. I follow. The place is painted dark red. The far wall is papered to look like a library. Platters of croissants and pastries are stacked up on the counter. My mind fastforwards and the doubts creep in. Once we've finished here, had our coffees, eaten our cakes, and I've hacked whatever it is Lucie's trying to get into, will that be that? This has happened before, people befriending me to do stuff for them. At school Joel was always calling me asking about our maths prep. But whenever he saw me in school, he avoided me as I wasn't part of his cool gang.

Lucie

We are the only customers in the cafe. Nav runs a speed test on the café's WiFi and then starts downloading apps for me. With one hand he taps into my phone and with the other drinks coffee and pulls apart a cinnamon swirl. He's oblivious to sugar dusting his black top. The pretty blonde waitress looks on and smiles.

"All the usual stuff is there: TikTok, Instagram, Snapchat, Gmail, WhatsApp, and Photoshop Express for your art." He hands me the phone. "Just sign in."

"Thanks," I say signing into my accounts. Thankfully these all have the same old Frida Kahlo password with no weird combinations of capitals and numbers!

"I need the *DNA Ancestor Heritage* app too," I add in my most carefree voice as if every teenager has it downloaded.

"No problem." He takes my phone and searches the App Store. "You wouldn't believe the weird combination of apps some people have."

Is Nav saying I'm weird? "What sort of apps?" I ask.

Nav blushes and I suppress the urge to laugh. "Can't say, he mumbles."

I don't pursue the question. It would be mean to make him blush again! I'm never going to be able to ask him to hack into my DNA account with Miss Pretty Waitress watching and listening as if we are her entertainment.

Luckily, a couple of women Mum's age come in and the waitress fires up the shiny Italian espresso machine. Phew! We're not alone. Then I have a moment of panic that Mum and her colleague Cherry will walk in. We're only round the corner from her office. I pray she's too busy at work to take a break.

Nav leans across the little wooden table and against the whistles and whirs, he whispers, "So what do you want me to hack?"

"Can you hack through two-step authentication?" I ask, our heads bowed in conspiratorial secrecy.

He pulls away and sits back in his chair. He folds his arms behind his head. "That's virtually impossible!"

"Oh. In the movies hackers can always get in after a couple of tries," I say hopefully.

"That's the movies for you! But it's all encrypted and you really do need access to the second device to intercept the code. Nav sees my disappointed face and goes quiet and thoughtful.

"Okay," he says eventually. "I suppose the first question to answer is how the code is generated." Nav's face is blank. He's calculating. "It's all down to the seed value—that's the first number in the code. I need to find out how that's generated first, and from there I can try to work out the algorithm that gives you the rest. After that I should theoretically be able to duplicate the original key generator..."

I nod. I'm doing my best to get what he's saying, yet it makes my brain ache. It takes me back to GCSE ICT with Mr Knights. How I ever got a B I don't really know!

"Really, it'd be easier to hack into their device if they're already signed in. People use phishing, you know, on emails? But I don't want to get involved..."

"I'm not asking you to do anything illegal." I say.

The women on the next table glance over as they discuss the décor in stage whispers. "A repeat pattern of antique books," says one.

"Yes, it's quite cosy, isn't it?" replies the other woman.

It's now or never. I am getting very edgy. I can't wait much longer to find out my results. To persuade Nav to help me get on to the site and collect my results I'm going to have to resort to telling him the truth. I'm going to have to explain all about the DNA test, my mysterious biological father, and hope that after hearing the full story he'll take pity on me and help. My stomach tightens. Where to begin? In whispers I tell him my family story.

There's a long moment of silence. It hangs heavy. I'm afraid that Nav doesn't want to be my friend anymore. Is there something wrong here? I've always wondered if there was something wrong with me. After all, Mum and Steve always look nervous when someone asks where I'm from. I fill the long silence, waiting for Nav's reaction, letting my mind play through possibilities and scenarios I usually try not to think about. Was my father awful to Mum? Did he have some genetic disease? Was he a criminal? Somehow today the nicer stories of him being a long-lost prince or famous for some amazing talent just won't come. Instead, I am flooded by a wave of negativity.

Finally, Nav smiles and says, "That's so cool!"

I explain how the results came in and I got locked out of the site before I could see them. He smirks. Why is he smirking? This is not a comedy. It is a tragedy. "Baring my soul isn't funny! It isn't a joke," I hiss.

"That's why you wanted your old phone! It's okay. May I?" he glances at my new mobile.

"Sure."

He takes my phone and opens the DNA app. "What's your email again?"

I tell him what now sounds a very childish email address. "Don't laugh, but it begins with Jucie Lucie! I was twelve when I made that and thought it was cool. I'm definitely going to have to change it before I go to art school."

Unable to conceal his amusement, he chuckles as he keys in the information.

"What are you doing?"

"Put in your password." He hands me the phone. "I used your sim card to set this up, so it's the same number. You should just get the code by text."

I follow Nav's instructions. Why didn't I think about this? It's so obvious. Of course Nav would transfer the sim card. *Of course* he didn't set me up with a totally new number! I feel like a total idiot. I guess I was too stressed to think straight. I log into the account. I pause, my finger hovering over the DNA results tab. Our eyes meet. He nods encouragingly and I press open. The results are in. My origins. My heritage is there in front of my eyes.

Nav

I explain why a pie chart is the best way to visualise DNA make-up. At first, Lucie's really listening, but then comes that glazed-over look I've noticed on some people when I explain mathematical concepts.

"I don't care how they've displayed the information. That's not the point!" Lucie looks troubled. "I need to get out of here," she says.

Like accomplices on the run, I pay up swiping my phone at the reader as we go. We walk quickly, purposefully, silently. I have no idea where we are going or what's really going on!

The sun has come through the mist and it feels like summer again! We find ourselves by the river and sit down on the wooden bench which already seems like our place; in the same way it used to be the go-to spot for me and Archie.

"How are you doing?" I ask.

"Good" Lucie says uncertainly. Then she says, "That's a lie...Sorry. I'm not too good...I feel really overwhelmed and fragile." After a long pause she mumbles, "I need to process things before I can say anything. Just talk to me."

I do as she asks and start chatting about the way she looks like she could be from so many places. This seems to cheer her up and she joins in sharing stories of being asked: *Where are you from?* Then the follow up question: *Where are you really from?* My mouth starts to run dry from all the talking and I consider asking if she wants to go to that cool bar again. What I really want to ask her is, "What are your DNA results? What did you find that made you react so strongly?"

Lucie's phone rings. "Sorry'" she says. "It's Maisie, my sister. 'What's up Mais?'"

I hear Maisie's every word. She speaks rapidly without stopping for breath. Maisie wants Lucie to send her some money so she can go to a tanning salon.

Lucie and my eyes meet in some kind of mutual understanding. We both have to deal with younger brothers and sisters.

"Mum will go mad if you do that!" says Lucie. "What makes you think I've got any money? It was Easter when I did my last shift at the pub." She ends the call.

"Maisie's asking me for money to get a tan. It's like some weird sick joke, asking this today of all days."

What does Lucie mean? I don't get why she's so annoyed with her sister. "Maybe she wants to look more like her big sister?" I suggest.

"Ugh" Lucie shakes her head.

"It's a crazy world we live in," I say suddenly getting it, getting why she's annoyed. "Half the world wants a tan and the other half wants to lighten their skin."

"What a crazy messed up world!" says Lucie.

A man walking along the riverside footpath with his dog, a pit bull terrier, stops abruptly. They both stare at us.

Nervous, I look away. Lucie stares them out. The dog tugs on its lead and man and dog are off and away.

"Why did you look away? Are you okay?" she asks.

"Second nature. I want to avoid trouble."

"What do you mean?" asks Lucie.

"When we first moved from Birmingham to Norfolk there was this really mean boy called Oscar Seward at my new primary school. He used to call me names like the P-word, and say I didn't wash and that was why my skin was a dirty brown. Sometimes he'd get the others to gang up on me too, so I'd spend most of playtime hiding in the boys' loo."

"That's terrible," says Lucie.

"Oscar Seward's dad used to come up to school with a dog just like that one. In fact, I think that man across the river *was* Mr. Seward."

We sit in silence for a moment.

"Didn't the teachers do anything?" asks Lucie.

"They said it was just a bit of banter."

"That's terrible."

"Eventually they developed a zero-tolerance policy on racism. But in this part of the country, where almost everyone is white, the kids only ever saw a black or brown face on television. There were definitely some days when I thought life would have been much easier if I looked just like the others."

"I totally get that," says Lucie.

Is she going to tell me?

I pause, but Lucie doesn't say anything so I keep talking. "To be honest most of the kids were pretty nice, but only in that they wouldn't get involved in the sorts of things Oscar and his mates would do. It's not like they ever actually defended me, or even just befriended me. I guess in some ways, they were part of the problem too, pretending they hadn't seen or heard anything."

"That's just crazy."

"I know." I look at Lucie. "So, are you going to tell *anyone* your results?" I ask, hoping that the *anyone* could be me.

Lucie takes a deep breath. "I'm really happy for you to be the first person to know." She takes out her phone and enlarges the pie chart. Now it's my turn to take a sharp intake of breath, but I try not to show my surprise.

"As expected, half of me is from Northern Europe—Scottish, Irish, Scandinavian—obviously on my mum's side. And the other half of me is South Asian. But unlike the Europe segment they don't say where from. Looking at this my father could be from anywhere from Nepal to Sri Lanka! It's a pretty big area."

"And a massive population, too. How does it feel, now you know you have ancestors from the Indian subcontinent, knowing where you are *really* from?" I ask.

"I don't know. I can't explain it. In a way I feel one hundred per cent better and at the same time it is as if nothing has changed at all."

"It'll take time to process," I say, thinking I sound like my father talking to one of his patients on the phone.

Lucie frowns. "I'm not really sure how to process this. I don't *feel* Indian, Scottish, or Irish…" she says.

"Did kids say mean things to you at school too?" I ask. "Is that why you did the test?"

"A bit, but it was the parents who were worse! At primary school I went home for tea to a girl called Suzanne's house. We were eating pizza when I heard her mum on the phone to a friend. 'Suzi's brought that half-caste girl home for tea.' I didn't know what half-caste even meant. But by the tone of her voice it sounded like something bad, and once again I felt different to everyone around me. I didn't dare tell Mum."

"I understand. I never told my parents about Oscar either," says Nav.

"When I looked half-caste up it in the dictionary it said it was a term for being of multiracial descent."

"Fair enough," says Nav.

"But wait for it. It comes from the Latin word *castus*, meaning pure. Or in my case, only half pure."

"Putting people into meaningless groups and then making racial slurs about them is a British Empire thing," I say.

"It happens everywhere. Divide and rule. Think about the civil rights movement in America or apartheid in South Africa."

"Yeah, you're right," I say, thinking I don't usually talk about these things with my mates. The only time these topics ever came up was at debating club.

"Have you ever thought about the way we divide people up when you make an application," says Lucie. "Have you filled out any forms or surveys, lately? There's always a long section at the end, sometimes taking up most of the form. It asks for *a bit about you*. Sex. Gender. Age. Physical or mental health and then the question: *To which ethnic group do you belong?*"

"Why do they really need to know?" I say. "Now you could answer with percentages. That would give the statisticians something to think about."

Lucie laughs.

"Seriously though," I continue, "highlighting people's differences, rather than looking for common ground is always a disaster waiting to happen. Although..."

"Go on," says Lucie.

"Another way to think about things is to accept that we are all part of so many tribes: cricket team, fantasy fiction fan, vegan, asthmatic (that's me), wheelchair user, the list goes on. This is the kind of thing my father says when he talks about his patients, about how, in order to get the full picture, he needs to take intersectionality into account—that's the way so many things, both big and small can marginalise people."

"That's so true. Your dad sounds really cool," says Lucie.

"He is the least cool person I know," laughs Nav. "He dresses like Mr. Adams from college: plaid shirts and beige chinos from Marks and Spencer."

Lucie smiles. "I don't really know what I think anymore. Everything is shifting," she says. Her eyes brighten. "Actually, you're right. It's like Brexiteers and Remainers grouping together in separate camps and becoming enemies. Mum avoids my nan after she voted for Brexit."

"My great-grandmother and her sister were divided by Partition. She was married to a Muslim and stayed in Pakistan and her sister who'd married a Hindu went to India. My great-grandmother in Gojra wrote a letter every week for forty years to her sister in Delhi."

I've never talked to anyone about this kind of thing. Archie's my best mate, I know everything he thinks about the latest Apple updates, but I'd never tell him about my family, not like this. Our conversations have never ventured into this terrain, and I don't think he'd understand.

Lucie nods. I think she wants me to continue. I'm learning to interpret her. Sometimes when I talk maths and science to people their eyes glaze over—like the pie chart incident in the café—and I know that's when I have to stop. "My great-grandma's letters continued through war, peace, births, deaths, marriages and weeks when nothing much happened. Same family. Different countries."

"Through war?" asks Lucie.

"The war with India. My great Uncle Iqbal was martyred in the civil war in 1971."

Lucie flinches.

I wonder why she flinched. Was it the word martyr? Does it sound too religious or political? "Punjabi to English doesn't translate martyr quite right and to be honest it is the sort of old-fashioned phrase my grandparents use. Let me think. A better translation is died in action—for God, King and country. And all that stuff."

Lucie smiles. "How many languages do you speak?"

"Punjabi as mother tongue. Some Urdu, French, German, and English of course. My mother's family often spoke English, even at home in Pakistan."

"English in Pakistan? How come?" Lucie asks.

"Alongside Urdu, it is the official language of Pakistan. British Empire and all that." I google Indian and Pakistani

96

languages for her. "Look it says India has 122 major languages and 1599 other languages! And 73 languages are spoken in Pakistan."

"Wow!" says Lucie. Although her expression doesn't look like she's impressed. Her mouth is turned down at the corners. She sighs.

"What's up?" I ask.

"I thought when I got the results, it would pinpoint an actual place that my father's ancestors came from. If I click on the coloured wedges for the European bit, it has details like Cheshire, or Northern Scandinavia. The South Asia half is a whole subcontinent and the more I think about it the more deflated I feel. It's so vague, even though the data comes from such an enormous area, with so many people, countries, cultures and so many languages."

"Maybe more Europeans and North Americans take the test. A bigger pool of data would allow for that difference. Also, there are several companies offering DNA tests. They each have a different pool of data and some might be more popular in some countries than others."

Lucie looks at me glumly. I'm not sure if she gets or believes my explanation. "There is one way to narrow it down," I tell her.

"Really? How?"

"You could move raw data, your personal and unique data, to a site that finds relatives."

"I see," says Lucie. I'm not sure she really gets what I am saying.

"What I mean is you will see people's names and where they are from. If nearly all your relatives are from, for example, Bangladesh—you'll know about your own ethnicity. Most likely scenario is you'll get some eighth cousin once removed as a match. But…" I pause, dramatically, "It will have details of where *they* are from."

"No way! That's amazing. You're amazing!" says Lucie. "How do I do it? Will I have to pay extra for that?"

"Usually, yes. But I know a site which will do it for free. We need a computer. I'll show you!"

Lucie

Visions of Nav visiting my house, in my bedroom sat with my laptop at my dressing table, run through my mind. Mum would be over-chatty, ask him a whole tonne of stupid questions and after he left, she would ask me a whole load more. Could I ever convince her that Nav and I are just friends, and that we're trying to track down my father and my origins? No way!

"We can go to mine?" suggests Nav. "There won't be anyone there until later tonight."

"Sure," I say, my stomach lurches. I'm suddenly scared of what we might find.

Nav

We walk through the underpass. No buskers today. I'm about to say, "Do buskers go on holiday?" when Lucie slows down in front of the murals.

"Want to guess which one's mine again?" she asks, remembering that I didn't manage to get the right answer last time.

I have a bad feeling about this. It's going to be like guessing an auntie's age when even the correct answer isn't the right! What if the mad-eyed supersize cat mural is Lucie's? Could I be friends with someone who created *that*? Then my eyes are drawn to the painting beside the hideous cat. It's made up of intricate yellow and red geometric shapes and it looks really familiar. Some of the diamonds are painted in gold and catch the light. I can't believe I never really noticed this painting before.

"Is that yours? It's my favourite," I say. I'm ready to be struck down for being both incorrect and having no artistic taste.

Lucie's face softens into a smile. If people could really glow—I'd say that at this moment in the gloomy subway Lucie is glowing. "Eureka! You got it! You, Nav Chowdery have very good taste."

No one has ever said that I have good taste! I start playing with the idea in my head. Perhaps when I go to uni I should branch out a bit and go to gigs, festivals, even exhibitions. I suddenly realise that I've been living in a very narrow world.

Lucie

On the main road heading out of town, the houses, trees, cars—everything in fact—grows bigger and smarter with every step. I'm bathed in the warm glow of Nav seeing me through my artwork. It sounds so unoriginal, but it is like hearing someone's playlist and realising it's just like yours. Pretty amazing to feel so connected. "How did you guess right?" I ask.

"I suppose really there was a one in thirty-six chance of getting it right," says Nav. "No. One in thirty-five as I'd used up one guess. There are four routes through the subway, and you've only ever asked when we're on this route so that makes it a one in seven chance."

I could be deflated. I could be consumed by my artistic ego, but I'm not. I love his quirky way of thinking. It is like a door into another world.

"And…" Nav stalls for a moment looking at me. "It really was my favourite…"

His favourite!

"…and there's something else you should know about it," he adds excitedly.

"What, something else?" I ask. At first I'm intrigued, but then I worry, *What if it's something critical that I don't want to hear?*

"Wait and see."

"See?" I mutter.

"Yes. Wait and see."

We turn into the gravel drive. An enormous Georgian three-storey house stares down at me. The ground floor windows are as tall as our front door! Are all of Nav's family super rich?

Nav unlocks the front door. It is painted duck-egg blue, the colour you see in seaside cafes or posh interior design shops. A quintessential English home. I'm about to share this thought but think better of it and stop myself. I follow Nav from his hallway into the lounge, my footsteps echoing on the wooden floor.

Nav keys in a security code. "I have to be quick or the alarm will go off!"

There's a silence. An awkward nervous silence anticipating what we're about to do. "It's not usually so peaceful here," says

Nav breaking the silence. "Muni and Nadiya, my younger brother and sister are staying with Aunty Mona in Manchester. Sometimes when there's aunts, uncles, cousins staying it's a madhouse. You can't hear yourself think. And sometimes my paternal grandparents come and stay for several months at a time too."

"Months?" I say, "Wow! Mum isn't on great terms with Nana Pat; an hour or two for Christmas, birthdays and the occasional Sunday lunch is as long as we get to see her for! Mum has a saying, 'Guests are like fish, they go off after three days!'"

Nav doesn't laugh.

"The grandparents went to Manchester last week and then will head off soon to the States for autumn."

"They're allowed to go to America? I thought they were really strict about visas. When my Nana Pat went on her trip of a lifetime to Florida, she had some issue getting a visa. Although knowing Nana Pat, maybe she just got in a muddle!"

"My grandparents have British passports. They first came over to the UK in the 1960s, back when it was the British Commonwealth and all that. Believe me, since 9/11 you can't go *anywhere* with a Pakistani passport," explains Nav.

"That's so unfair," I say.

"Some people think we're all terrorists. Do you know which passport is the best? The one you need least visas to travel the world with?"

"No...um...British?" I guess.

"A German passport, followed by a Singaporean one," says Nav.

"Really?"

"Yes. You can check all this out online," says Nav earnestly. I nod.

"I want to show you something." Nav leads me into the dining room. The large windows and wooden floor are of ballroom proportions! At the far end is a large dining table. On the wall above it instead of the typical still life or landscape painting (or arty photograph in our house), is a large wall hanging. TV makeover shows would call it a feature wall. Geometric diamonds and zigzags are embroidered in yellow and red. Light shines in through the French windows and catches the threads, lighting them up as if they are made from copper and gold.

Nav stares at me and back at the hanging. "What do you make of this? Rather like your mural design."

"I like it," I say coolly, trying not to reveal how spooked I feel. I know there's nothing original in art, but...

"It started life as a shawl but it's too fragile to be worn."

"I've seen Persian rugs displayed like this," I say.

"It's pretty old. An antique. My great-grandparents were in the textile business. Here, look! This is them."

Lined up on the piano is a set of framed family photographs. A collection of faces capturing a moment in time stare out through the glass of mismatched wood and metal frames. Posed and staged black and white images of grandparents and great-grandparents segue into high-contrast Kodak prints from the late 60s and early 70s. Holiday snaps: on the beach, a group at the gates of Buckingham Palace. Year by year school photographs of Nav and his brother and sister. Graduation pictures: a man and a woman posing in black gowns and with mortar boards on their heads. They look younger than us.

The only thing which links these people through different times and places is their shared bloodline. Their shared DNA. Their shared heritage is what this line up is all about. This overt display of the desire to preserve the knowledge of who made us who we are, stings and brings into sharp contrast my lack of a line-up of pictures to give me history, roots, family.

For a moment I think of Mum's amazing photos. She travelled the world capturing the faces of musicians, dancers, businessmen, nomads, and women with henna tattoos. Nav's grandparents wouldn't look out of place in her albums.

Our family pictures are all displayed in the alcove in the lounge. Mum and Dad's wedding day, Maisie and me at school, a few holiday snaps. My face stands out. I just don't fit in with their fair hair and fair skin. If a stranger had to place me in Nav's family or mine—they'd choose his. I guess it shouldn't bother me, but sometimes it does.

One photograph draws me in, and I can't seem to take my eyes off the couple. "Who are they?" I ask.

"My great-grandparents."

If I was like Jenny and good at painting portraits, this charismatic couple would be my first choice. There's something about them. They are both dressed in white; this contrasts dramatically with their dark hair and skin. Chiaroscuro is the technical term used by art critics to describe the contrast.

I once used the word chiaroscuro to fend off an unwanted comment about my appearance. A couple of months ago I was at the bus stop. A guy I'd never seen before asked me if it stopped at Plaxton. I explained that it did, but it was a request stop. "Thanks," he said. "Has anyone told you what lovely white teeth you have?"

"Really," I said, truly unaware that my teeth were any whiter, any brighter than anyone else's in the queue.

"All of you lot do," he said.

It took a moment to dawn on me that he was talking about the contrast of my white teeth against my brown face. The same as he'd seen on other black, brown and mixed-race people who he lumped together as some homogenous group called "you lot".

"Chiaroscuro," I said, playing the part of the intellectual art critic, using an originally Italian word which means light-dark to deflect the racist comment. Looking back, that day was one of the many small events which propelled me on to the DNA test.

Nav

Lucie is staring at my family photos as if they're some kind of exhibit in a museum, specimens up for scrutiny. "There's so many of them!" says Lucie. She's far more interested in them than the shawl or in getting on with her DNA upload.

"Just the immediate family. It doesn't include the cousins. Dad has thirty-two."

"Wow! Mum only has three cousins and we hardly ever see them. Everyone is always too busy to meet up." Lucie points at one of the photos. "Who are they, at the foot of the Eiffel Tower?"

"Mum and Dad on their honeymoon in Paris."

Lucie looks at Mum in the same questioning way she looked at my great-grandparents. "Mum cringes at her flicked-back hair and blue eye-shadow now." I laugh.

"Late twentieth-century style," says Lucie gravitating back to the picture of my mum's parents.

"They had the textile business." I point to the shawl. "Do you see what I meant earlier?"

"Did your grandma make it?" asks Lucie.

"Not sure. The tradition is that a grandmother begins the shawl when a baby is born. But I'm not sure exactly who made this one," I say.

"It's so clever," says Lucie.

"Women traditionally learnt to sew as kids. They were highly skilled. That's why so many of them came to the UK to work in the textile industries."

"Did yours?"

"No! My family owned the factories."

"Get you!" laughs Lucie. "The rich boy."

I hate it when people have a go at you for things you can't change: skin colour, hair colour, family, money.

"We should get to work! We need to upload your DNA." I boot up my laptop on the dining room table. I talk through the whole procedure with Lucie. I am aware that I'm rushing like I used to when Joel would ring after school wanting me to explain our maths homework. But I want to get to the interesting bit! Lucie has logged into her account and I transfer the genetic code into a zip file. "I'm saving your unique raw DNA on to my hard drive. It's the only way we can then transfer it. Is that okay?"

She nods.

"I'll keep it safe and then delete it. You can't be too careful. And don't get your hopes up too much, it'll be less vague than the results you got, but you probably won't find anything definite either."

"What do you mean? I thought they did all kinds of DNA tests these days to confirm paternity and so on."

"Sure, but the results show likelihood, not a definitive answer. For example, a man could come up as being related to you, with say a twenty-one per cent DNA match." Lucie's nodding, following along. "That would mean the man could be your half-brother or your uncle. It's only when you piece other data together, like dates of birth and so on that you then decide if the man is your half-brother or your uncle."

"I think I get it," says Lucie.

I'm not sure if I have explained it well enough. I'm tempted to try again and give some actual examples like in a biology lesson. Instead I continue to talk in what I hope is a light chatty way. "Scientific tests can rule things out, though. That someone *isn't* your mother or father due to blood type. Now I just need to set you up on DNAcademia.org."

"What's that?" asks Lucie.

"It's the name of the organisation that is working on a DNA project at the university where my mum works. Apparently it is a massive project with partner universities all over the world."

I login on the site and then hit the first problem. Before you can upload the data, you have to complete a timed online IQ test. I guess that's how we can access the site for free. I shouldn't be surprised. This DNA site is all about mapping intelligence. The good thing is, I love IQ tests. I scroll through the first section of true/false questions at lightning speed.

"What are you doing?" asks Lucie. "Are you playing a game?"

"I just…sort of…" I mumble. "Nearly there. Such easy questions: if a triangle is three, a glove is five, a bicycle is two. What is a clock? Twelve of course!" I'm on a roll until I get to a question I need to think about.

"Artist and scientist, vindaloo and rice," says Lucie reading out the question. "Easy, Leonardo da Vinci."

"Wow!" I say clicking the final answer. "We're in." I upload Lucie's raw data. "All done!"

Lucie looks at me nervously as if bracing herself for the results. A message arrives on the screen:

It may take five to seven days for your DNA matches to be visible. We will be in touch later this year with the project's final findings.

"I don't believe it!" says Lucie. "I thought it would churn out the data in minutes. It can't be that complicated."

"It *is* complicated. Trust me. It's only in our lifetimes, in the last few years actually, that the human race has been able to find any of this out and that science has made this possible. You've waited all these years to know. What's another week?" I say, trying to put it in perspective. "You'll get an email notification."

"When the results come through, will you look at them with me?" asks Lucie.

"Sure," I say. This makes me feel slightly nervous. What if she gets emotional, teary, and weird? I won't know what to do. At least this isn't the kind of DNA test where you find out all kinds of medical nasties. "I'll see you in a week, or less hopefully!" I say shutting down the laptop.

"Am I dismissed?" says Lucie with a smirk.

"Yes, class dismissed" I chuckle. It feels nice to joke around a bit. I've never found anyone I can talk to like this, really honestly and about all kinds of things.

"Okay. Thanks," says Lucie standing up and looking back up at the wall hanging.

A thought crosses my mind. *Maybe people do inherit tastes, predispositions to all kinds of things. Do I like Lucie's mural more than the others because it reminds me of our wall hanging— which would be nurture? Or is it because Mum's family were in the textile business for years and a liking for certain patterns and colours is in my genes? How could you ever prove it either way?*

The kitchen door rattles. "Cooey!" calls a voice.

Lucie and I both jump.

"Hi, Di." I say to the cleaning lady.

Lucie

Dad is in the kitchen throwing some basil leaves, grated cheese and nuts into the food processor. I realise I'm starving.

"Smells good," I say over the whir.

"Spaghetti with homemade pesto," shouts Dad. He spoons the green sauce into a bowl. "Just us three for dinner tonight."

"Is Maisie out?" I ask.

"No. Mum's at her book club," says Dad.

"Oh, yeah. She did tell me."

Dad takes the pan over to the sink and drains the pasta. "Maisie!" he shouts up the stairs.

When I was younger Mum's book club night was always the best night of the week. Dad made a massive dinner and then we'd slob out on the sofa and watch catch up episodes of *The Great British Bake Off.* The show is a bit too reality TV for Mum, but we love it. I'm sure that's where Dad got some of his cake ideas from! I place the familiar blue handled cutlery and white hexagonal plates on the table.

"Where's Mum?" asks Maisie bounding into the kitchen.

"Book club," says Dad placing the serving bowls in the middle of the table.

"I don't think they actually read any of their books! They just get together and eat and drink and talk," says Maisie dishing out equal portions of delicious smelling pasta and sauce.

"That's fine by me," says Dad. "They probably gossip about us! But it's good to let off some steam. Let's eat before this cools down."

"You're quiet, Lucie," says Maisie.

"Got my mouth full," I splutter, which is technically true. I also feel a bit of an imposter here, like I am leading a double life. My familiar life at home with Mum, Dad and Maisie; and then my new life where my DNA tells me I also belong elsewhere. I can't see how the two parts of me are ever going to come together.

Tori

The narrow roads are crammed with cars. Finally, I manage to reverse into the tiniest of spaces. It is always like this when we meet at Cherry's terraced house in the city. Sometimes I'm envious of the fact that my colleague and friend has only a ten-minute walk to work, whereas I have to drive everywhere. Then again, I'm not the one who complains all day if I'm forced to give up my parking spot.

I ring the bell.

Cherry opens the door and smiles broadly. Always one for wearing dresses at work or play, she is in an orange and pink floral number and matching fuchsia-coloured high heels. We kiss on the cheek. "We're out the back, in the garden."

Down the long hall and into the backyard we go. It is filled with plant pots and an assortment of mismatched garden furniture topped with brightly coloured cushions. She hands me a glass of orange juice and I dunk crisps into the hummus dip. The whole gang is here. Hilary who is now retired from the art school, Cara and Rachel who lecture on the Fine Art degree, and Cherry's neighbour Shathy, a primary school teacher.

We share our children's A-level results and holiday stories. "Glad I'm done with all that," says Hilary, who is a few years older than the rest of us. "Nowadays it's the grandchildren I have to think about, and what's more I can holiday outside of term time!" For the briefest of moments I wonder if I will ever have grandchildren. I can't imagine Lucie and Maisie having children of their own.

After an hour or so of drinking and chatting, Cherry says, "We'd better talk about the book."

Remembrance of Things Past by Marcel Proust is not a book I would have chosen. But the book club is a democracy and it got the most votes when we met last time. We all had the idea that we wanted to read something more challenging. And I guess the whole point of a book club is to read stories you wouldn't normally choose.

Cherry holds up her hardback copy. "*Remembrance of Things Past* is not necessarily the remembrance of things as they were," she says reading from the book.

"You can say that again!" Everyone turns to me and laughs, except for Cherry. I'm not sure if I was meaning to be funny. With Lucie on the point of leaving home I've been thinking about my past.

"Better to forget the past!" says Hilary, "I don't want to remember too much—I'm on my third marriage!"

Cherry lectures in Film Studies and likes a good debate, so is ruffled by our light tone. The rest of us have resorted to being typical teachers let off the leash. We can't but help ourselves act out the role of unruly students!

Later on, after Hilary leaves to collect one of her step-children from the train station and Cherry switches on the fairy lights, the tone changes. In the semi-darkness we talk more seriously about our trouble with the past.

It is the perfect moment, amongst good friends, for me to share something about Lucie's biological father. About that difficult part of my past which is increasingly haunting me. But I just can't bring my nebulous thoughts to words. It's like wading through fog. For this part of my past feels like somebody else's story. And that somebody else was packed away in a locked box and the key thrown away. *Move forward* was always my motto. But maybe that was never completely true or possible. I've always had one foot in the past—Lucie is evidence of that. I have to talk to Lucie about her biological father before she leaves for art school. *But how?*

"Are you alright, Tori?" asks Cherry. "You seem lost in thought."

"I am lost in the past," I confess. "You can never really shake it off. You know as you get older, events which seemed buried forever suddenly pop up as if from nowhere."

"They say that gets even more pronounced when you're really old," says Cherry.

"We've all got that to look forward to," laughs Cara, the youngest of us in her early forties.

"I'm not talking about dementia. Before my mother passed away, she could remember things in great detail about her youth. How she met my father, and even old boyfriends I never knew about," continues Cherry.

A shiver passes down my spine.

Shathy leans forward. "Apparently, the people we meet and events which happen in our late teens and early twenties are somehow hard-wired into our brain. We had a lecture about it at teacher training but my memory is hopeless and I can't remember much, especially this late at night!" She yawns. "It's a good job I only live next door!"

"I know what you mean," I reply. "It's like how most of us still have close friends from those days and we might not speak for months, but when we do the bond is still there."

"Exactly. All part of our psychology and nothing to be embarrassed or ashamed about," says Cherry. "If you're thinking about something or someone from your past, it must be important to you now. It's better not to ignore it or it'll eat away at you."

Cherry's right. I breathe a sigh of relief and silently vow to talk to Lucie about her biological father as soon as possible.

Saturday 20th August

Maneer

I turn to face the clock. Almost half past five. My family mock me for using an old-fashioned analogue clock when I could set an altogether more pleasant alarm on my phone: birdsong, David Bowie, Queen—sounds I've loved for years. It's hard to break habits of a lifetime—waking early to the trusty clock face that stands on my bedside table and listening to my music heroes on vinyl are just a few of them. *Am I getting too old to change any of my ways?* I wonder. Weekdays I am always the first up. I recite my prayers—another habit?—and am out of the house and at my desk before Marg, our receptionist, officially opens the surgery.

Light peeps in around the edge of the bedroom curtains. It's a Saturday, and Maryam likes to sleep in so I compromise and never set the alarm at the weekend. Nevertheless, my internal clock is set for an early start.

As a boy my lark-like circadian rhythm was a definite advantage. I'd be up and out on my bike delivering newspapers around the streets of Bolton and back in time to open the shop, helping myself to a carton of sweet Ribena and a packet of crisps for breakfast. A day's work already done, when my bleary-eyed mother would come down from the flat above and take over the shop. A mad dash for school. Where, although I don't like to boast, I have to say, I excelled at maths and science. I kept my head down and got on. The teachers said I was a model pupil. I don't think any of them were aware that outside of the classroom I was quite different. I had to develop a thick skin and a sense of humour, both ignoring and deflecting the name calling. It was a matter of my physical and mental survival.

After school I'd spread out my textbooks on the shop counter and do my homework. I even revised for my O-levels between serving customers. I rose above everyone's wildest expectations. To their great joy, they were finally going to have a doctor in the family. I was the embodiment of every immigrant family's dream. And what's more, I was the proud and lucky recipient of a full grant which saw me through medical school in London.

It was there, at King's College, that I rebelled. A bit late for a general teenage rebellion—but I had no time for that until then for I was either working or studying! My rebellion was very specific; it was about one thing only. It took some time before I faced my parents and told them the thing I'd been skirting around on each visit home. How to tell them that I wanted to marry out? To marry a woman of my choice? "Just tell them!" my friends advised. I desperately wanted to tell my family about how I wished to marry one specific woman. The woman in question was beautiful and educated; someone who could be my equal, my life partner.

But I didn't dare say any of that. So, my parents set the matchmakers to work, and I forced myself out on several dates with nice enough girls, but always refused to go on a second date. What a waste of everybody's time! There were even suggestions about marrying a distant cousin from the ancestral village. I was aghast at this thought: I would have nothing in common with her! I don't just mean education-wise. All those other things which were important to me: listening to my vinyl collection, foreign language films where you can never guess the ending, my opposition to the government talk of abolishing grants. That was all part of me.

In the end, I had no choice but to drop the bombshell. The thing was, I'd found the woman I would marry. The woman was Maryam. I was calm, measured and lightened the blow by telling them that I wasn't talking about marrying an English girl.

A Desi girl—the term for the Indian subcontinent's diaspora—would tick all the boxes.

A few months back I was at a conference in Edinburgh, I had seen the word Desi used on a restaurant menu. Along with all the Dopiazas and Kormas there was a separate section entitled Desi.

"What's Desi?" asked an elderly colleague.

"Traditional cooking," I said.

He nodded.

Then after a moment I wanted to say more. "It's more than a section on a menu!" I explained how Desi refers to the people, cultures, and traditions of the Indian subcontinent and their diaspora. About how the term was derived from ancient Sanskrit meaning homeland.

I couldn't restrain myself from ordering *Lahori Chana*, that delicious comfort food of chickpeas in gravy. Simple home cooking. I'd abstained from choosing *Maghaz* for my main. The menu described it as melt in the mouth. "Probably best to order from the main menu," I advised the others. The pan cooked sheep brain would have been be a step too far for my curry loving colleagues. *Or is it that my tastes have become more British, too?* I wondered. I am someone who is sometimes British, sometimes Pakistani.

Maryam tosses and turns pulling the duvet towards her. Last night I suggested we go out for Saturday lunch. I wanted a chance to discuss my concerns about Nav. The other day when he told me he was going to start studying for Cambridge, I told him to relax for a bit. I didn't want him to burn out with all that studying.

"Nav's fine," she said, looking away and hastily adding that she had to go into work and would call if she was finished by noon. She then added that it was a special project she was working on with Mathilde. I know how much mutual respect there is between Maryam and her colleague. I like Mathilde's confidence and lack of interest in other people's opinions about her. I find it an attractive and enviable trait. Nevertheless, I know Maryam, and she wasn't telling me the whole truth. For a moment I wondered if she really was meeting Mathilde. I felt the same way I do when I know my patients are not telling the full story. The obese who swear they live on rice cakes and the alcoholics who swear they only drink a few units a week. There's nothing to do but wait until they tell me more.

It's too early to get up so I let my mind drift and think of work. A few weeks ago I was in the corridor at the surgery and overheard Marg, the receptionist, say to the pharmacist—who was waiting for me, "Dr. Chowdery knows how to ask the patients things another way, and although he's always running late, he gets to the heart of the matter." I'd smiled at the compliment. And from Marg of all people! She's always a bit abrasive to patients on the phone. They are quite scared of her. Me too sometimes!

I waited for Maryam to tell me more about her project with Mathilde. But she said nothing. No comment. Over the years I've noticed how Maryam's brain works on a different plane from most people. A strange combination of simplicity, almost naïvety in many matters and a sharp, clear mind that would send me into a nervous panic if I were one of her undergraduate students. That's what I love about her.

Nav takes after his mother in so many ways. Maryam and Nav are two peas in a pod, their heads whirring with numbers, data, and ideas; whilst I work with the people behind the data.

Yesterday, I waited in the house for Maryam to take her bicycle from the garage and leave. Marg could open the surgery, that is part of her job description. I'd wanted to talk to my son. Man to man. He seems so young, maybe too young, to be going away to university. So unworldly-wise.

By the time I was Nav's age I'd met every type of person. I'd had no choice. The whole world came to the corner shop. Mrs. Milton would cough and wheeze into the shop for her packet of Silk Cut cigarettes and tell me—still a teenager—all her woes. Like clockwork, Old Harry, who probably wasn't that old at all, would limp into the shop on the dot of 8am, dressed smartly in his pinstripe suit to buy his copy of *The Daily Mirror* and return to his two-up, two-down terraced house to spend a day alone with his memories.

I never reported Julie Pickles' after-school shoplifting. She had a thing for strawberry flavour Angel Delight. If I'm being honest, I had a soft spot for her, unlike her brother Mark. I can still hear Mark Pickles jeering me from the playground, "Here comes the P*** boy." For the briefest of moments, I'm tempted to turn my phone on and google Mark Pickles and Bolton and see what became of my nemesis. *Let it go!* I tell myself. In any case, those long hours in the shop set me up well for life as a General Practitioner where I see the world in any one extraordinary, ordinary morning. I was a "people person" before the term had been invented!

Having a conversation with your own family is another thing altogether. I have the knack of breaking through the usual teenage grunts and silences of my patients. Mothers and sons arrive weighed down with sad tales: depression, isolation, self-harm and usually leave a little lighter. It's simple there: you just reach out to that person.

However, nothing's so simple with my own wife and children. It would be much easier if they came to talk to me in the surgery. I'd feel far more at home and comfortable. Up until now, I've always been lucky with Nav. I enjoy our little chats about whatever he's read in *New Scientist,* or the YouTube tutorial he has watched.

Something has changed in Nav recently. Perhaps he's anxious about going to Cambridge. Over the summer I've already seen several teenagers and their mothers fearful about leaving home for university. I've diagnosed both mothers and teenagers with separation anxiety. Or perhaps Nav's found himself a girlfriend? Meeting Maryam was my turning point. I try to stop worrying and let my mind drift off back into a deep sleep.

Maryam

Last night Maneer asked me if I fancied driving out to the coast and having lunch at the famous fish and chip café on the pier today. I made the usual excuse; work. But this trip into work is different. I couldn't face telling my husband the purpose of it. A while ago Mathilde, the head of the biological psychology department, sent a round robin email to the whole faculty. The subject header read: *Is intelligence determined by genetics?* Intrigued, I opened the email. *Nature vs. Nurture. Join the debate. Be the debate.* In small print it asked for volunteers: all ages, genders and ethnicities were sought for IQ and DNA tests. The project was being run in conjunction with universities in Antwerp, Mumbai, Kyoto and Brisbane. Mathilde had followed it up with a personal message asking me if she could call upon my services to ratify some of the data analysis.

Normally I'd run a mile from others people's research projects, especially when connected to the notion of IQ. Not this time. I admire Mathilde. There is a mutual respect and friendship between us. I replied to Mathilde almost immediately saying, "Count me in!"

Even today, women working in mathematics and science are still very much part of a male dominated world. But each year there are more of us. It took me so long to get a permanent position at a university. I'd applied for so many jobs all across the country. I was on the point of giving up when the position came up in Norwich, a city I'd never even visited until my interview, though I'd heard enough about it from my brother to feel like I had. I knew I would love it and leapt at the opportunity. Luckily, being married to a GP means Maneer can get a job almost anywhere! So that's how we moved from Birmingham to Norfolk.

There's another reason that I was intrigued by Mathilde's project. Since having children, I have become increasingly interested in the nature versus nurture debate. I know that other parents have called me pushy, especially with Nav, who sat his GCSE maths in the first year of high school. This just isn't true. I am not pushy, but I fiercely believe that everyone should be able to reach their full potential.

I couldn't tell Maneer that I volunteered for this particular project. We've been together for over twenty years, long enough for me to know his opinion on the topic. My husband is cautious of such testing and data. For him intelligence is more a moral and ethical debate. I can hear Maneer now, citing the loss of millions of lives in horrors bought about by ethnic cleansing based on racial profiling as reason enough to not get involved. The Holocaust of six million Jews by the Nazis may be part of history, but the killing and displacement of the Rohingya Muslims in Myanmar by the Burmese is happening in the twenty-first century. All good reason to steer clear of such research.

My husband deals with the nature versus nurture debate on a daily basis. These days the job of a GP is health visitor, dietician, Job Centre, grandparent and social worker all rolled into one. He supports and nurtures people to reach their full potential.

This is the first time for many years that I have kept something from Maneer. Our marriage has always been an honest partnership; a marriage of equals. Except, there's just one thing I've never been able to talk to him, or anyone else about. An old wound I've kept hidden from Maneer for all these years. I like to justify my secrecy with the caveat: it all happened before we met. It was another time; a different time. I ruminate about the thing that has been lost and buried for so long, almost twenty years, sometimes rising to the surface and taking me by surprise when my eyes well up watching a film, or a conversation takes a particular turn. I truly hate these moments, hate these surprises which enter my brain unbidden. I am far more comfortable, more at home, with the binary surety of mathematics.

But this is the thing. The thing which Maneer and I could debate forever—and hence my reticence to discuss Mathilde's project. All scientific discoveries can lead to good or evil. The science itself is neutral. Science can save you. *The Martian* is mine and Nav's favourite film. Maneer watched the film with us the first time round and continually interrupted with comments about the way the character was unbelievable, and no one would be that mentally resilient left alone on Mars. "The astronaut would have gone crazy," complained Maneer. But that was entirely missing the point! The astronaut stranded on Mars uses maths, biology, chemistry and physics to stop himself from going crazy. To save himself.

Lucie

Now that my university place is confirmed, there are a whole load of forms to complete. I get to the final page and find the dreaded equality and diversity monitoring section. I usually tick decline to answer. Perhaps I should do as Nav suggested and fill in each of my percentages in the *Other* box.

"Do you need any help?" asks Mum wafting through the lounge.

I click on a new window.

"Or just my credit card details?" she sighs.

This could be the moment to bring up the topic of my ethnicity. I could ask all light and airily, "Which section should I fill in here?" But I still can't bring myself to ask her. "I'm good," I mutter.

Mum looks suspiciously at my phone as if I've been surfing inappropriate sites. "Is that new?" she asks.

"Yeah," I mutter.

"How did you pay for that?" Mum pauses. "I said I'd get you a new phone. Did you use the money from Nana Pat? How much money did Nana Pat give you for your birthday?"

"I used a bit of my birthday money and my savings," I lie, not wanting to get involved with one of Mum and Nan's recent fall outs or reveal just how generous Nana Pat has been. "The shop couldn't repair it, and this was on offer. There was a deal if I got it straight away." *Why can't I tell her that Nav gave me it as an apology, a replacement for breaking my phone? Isn't that what people do?* Part of me wishes I'd said all this on Thursday. But I couldn't and now it's too late.

Mum and I seem to live dodging around our secrets unable to say the things we need to say. I really want to say, "I do know which of those boxes to tick. I've had a DNA test. Tell me where in this enormous Indian subcontinent my father is from? Which sperm donor place did you use?" But I don't say any of that.

"Okay, well at least you've got a functioning phone," says Mum heading into the kitchen. There's a clatter of breakfast bowls going into the dishwasher. In the background *Woman's Hour* blasts out from the radio. They're interviewing a woman about surrogate tourism in India. This makes my stomach churn. Did Mum go to India to find a sperm donor? She did all that travelling stuff: from visiting the Taj Mahal to Thailand and on to New Zealand.

I get up and go into the kitchen. I'm ready to say something about surrogates and sperm donors, except the programme has moved on. The moment has gone. The radio blasts out a tune from a singer-songwriter who is being interviewed about her latest album. I stand by the counter. I steal a couple of chocolate digestives from the biscuit tin. Mum's brandishing a knife chopping up carrots and onions for the slow cooker.

I go back to my place on the sofa. If I can't have these conversations with Mum, I'm going to have to find out for myself. The DNA test was only the first step. Next step is to google sperm donor clinics in India and London. There must be some freedom of information, some details I can find out. I could tell them I'm unable to fill in this form for university. These tick boxes are very specific. Am I British-Bangladeshi, British-Indian, British-Pakistani, British-Nepali? Ironically, if you judge these things by the data, I am not actually British at all. My European part (Mum's side—I'm assuming!) is mostly Irish and Scandinavian. How come they don't have a Viking or Scandinavian section? How much of each place do you have to have in your DNA to fill this in? Nav is right with his idea of percentages. It makes racial profiling a little crazy.

I send Nav a message.

> Lucie: Hey

Nav: Hey

> Lucie: What are you up to today?

Nav: Helping in the workshop.

Nav: Any news from the match site?

> Lucie: No. Not yet!

Nav: Got to go. A bit busy.

> Lucie: Okay. Speak soon.

Nav

As an unofficial member of staff, I hide out in the workshop; this leaves Archie to deal with the Saturday morning queue which reaches as far as the shop door. I turn my phone to silent, as I need to focus on a whole stack of urgent repairs. I'm happy to work for free; after all I bartered my time to pay for Lucie's new phone. I like being busy in the back room at *Gadget Fix*, I feel completely at home solving puzzles, which for me is what each repair is. Maybe

I could work here permanently? I push the thought aside, as it merges with other thoughts of my parents' horror and disappointment if I passed on going to Cambridge and spent my days here.

Maneer

I wake. The bedside clock says a quarter past ten. *What's going on?* I never go back to sleep in the day. I've missed *subh* prayer! I trust Allah to give me lion-like strength to face the day, yet as I sit up my head feels foggy as if I have jet lag.

I pad downstairs in my slippers and bath robe. The house is empty. Silent. *Where is everyone?* In this rare moment of aloneness, it occurs to me that my life has always been one of being surrounded by others—the big extended family or work colleagues. For a moment I don't know what to do next. Nobody is asking me to do anything at all. My life is so different, so unimaginable to many of my lonely patients. The mothers raising children single-handedly. The elderly and those that live alone who have no one except for themselves to think about. I often suggest they get a pet which usually dampens down their hypochondria, most often fuelled by internet searches to pseudo-medical sites. Stroking a pet gives a glimmer of love and intimacy in their isolated lives. If I were Minister of Health, a pet on prescription would be my first policy change. A while back I'd found myself reading Nadiya's (the animal lover in the household) book, *A Street Cat Named Bob*. The cat, Bob, gave the homeless busker's someone to look after, to look out for, and to love unconditionally.

"Think of others" has always been my family's mantra. My sister Mona has really taken it to heart. It was instilled into us as children. I think of my sister's visit, bringing Nadiya and Muni back home for a couple of days. My selfless sister who drives down from Manchester and performs so much of the family's childcare through the long summer holidays. She sometimes seems more of a mother to my children than Maryam. I miss Nadiya and Muni. I wish they were here right now running around the house. I can't wait to see them. A physical longing forms in the pit of my stomach, a little like homesickness.

I need to be the sensible and pragmatic Dr. Chowdery everyone relies on, but I don't know where he's gone this morning. I thought I'd like a whole unobligated day ahead of me, but it is giving me a dose of melancholia. Best not to think too deeply about things, I tell myself, or I am going to end up wasting the whole day. But still the thoughts come. For a moment I even wish I was on-call so there was something I had to do, rather than trying to decide what I want to do. I wish the children were at home. I wish Maryam was at her desk in the study rather than at the university.

I'll make the house nice for when Maryam gets back, I think wandering through the pristine house on the lookout for the very occasional piece of clutter; an ordered house is one we can relax in. The only problem is that the house is clean and tidy already, so I resort to looking under furniture. I retrieve a tennis ball and an earring from under the sofa. It's in the shape of a silver teardrop, the one I bought Maryam as a stocking-filler last Christmas. I never really think about our marriage, we just get on with things. It was different when we were young; it was all-consuming to have fallen in love with a girl above my social standing even when we married back in the mid-nineties.

It was a miracle that the marriage happened at all. My family were hard to win round. They fussed, made idle threats, objections. Surprisingly, Maryam's parents readily agreed. She said it was because she was marrying every immigrant parent's dream; a doctor, an important man. I believed her. Although, right until the wedding day itself I had a nagging, fearful feeling that her parents had agreed too quickly and may just change their minds at the last minute.

Our children have had it so much easier. I can't imagine any of them working in a shop every day before and after school. I move the cushions around on the sofa and find a black rolled-up sock ball. Probably Nav's! I think about Nav going to Cambridge, it was so different for me, being the first in my family to go to university.

Maryam

I peddle harder. This morning, the ride out towards the university is a joy. The late summer sun warms my face and there isn't a car in sight. I feel exhilarated. On top of the world! I can even hear bird song. I must cycle more. Maybe we could do a family cycling weekend in September. Nav, Nadiya and Muni together one last time before he goes to university. But then again, it is the fact that it is just me and my bike that I love.

A dog walker with three small poodles steps out from the woods. I brake. "Glorious morning," says the woman.

I smile. "Perfect day." They all walk over the zebra crossing and everything feels right with the world.

A hundred metres on, I signal left and turn into Chancellor's Drive. No one is coming or going into the grey concrete buildings, which resemble ancient Mayan ziggurats. The campus is deserted except for the occasional international student who has stayed on over the summer. In a few weeks the place will be teeming with families dropping off their fresh-faced first years.

I check the time on my Fitbit. I'm early so I allow myself to freewheel, rolling along on the bike without having to turn the pedals I arrive at the lake exhilarated. I feel youthful, student-like, rather than a middle-aged woman. A couple of fishermen sit patiently in their deckchairs, their eyes fixed ahead on the glistening water. I consider staying here by the lake, relaxing. Isn't that what "normal" people who have hobbies do at the weekend?

Or am I procrastinating? Am I actually nervous about going in to see my colleagues in the research centre? It is impossible to second guess what they will tell me. Is this how Maneer's patients feel sitting in the surgery waiting room before being called in to hear test results: a heart condition, dementia gene, breast cancer... I don't usually think about myself. I don't usually put myself into the equation or data.

The grey concrete biological science block is closed. Shut for the weekend. Unlike many of my colleagues, who criticise the building's Brutalist design and say it reminds them of a 1970s car park, I like the bold stark lines. I'd prefer to live in a modernist house. But as it was Maneer who had to compromise when we moved here for my job, his choice of a traditional Georgian town house won out. His interest in architecture looks backwards, where I think I have something in common with my brother, Nabeel, looking forwards at more futuristic building design. Once, when I was Nav's age I'd briefly toyed with the idea of using my mathematical and problem-solving skills to train as an architect, but the call of pure, rather than applied mathematics won out.

I message Charlie to let him know I'm at the door. A minute later a smiling blue-eyed young man opens the door. I almost don't recognise the PhD student. His usual wayward curly hair has recently been closely cropped.

"Best bring it inside," says Charlie eyeing up my smart Pashley bicycle.

I wheel it inside and leave it at the bottom of the stairwell and follow Charlie upstairs. The view from the top floor of the campus, as far as the lake, is stunning. All bright and light. The fishermen are still in position, just as I left them.

"Just me and Mathilde up here today," says Charlie. Mathilde is a Nobel Prize nominated scientist. *Masters of their own little kingdom*, I think.

Mathilde shuffles her way towards us. Her navy T-shirt bears porridge stains, and her lank greying hair is pinned back by a multitude of mismatched hair grips. The sort of accessories— pink, blue and polka dot—my daughter, Nadiya now into her teens, has already grown out of. The first time I met Mathilde I thought the woman was a bag lady, a homeless woman, who'd stumbled past security. Later, I'd chastised myself for my stereotypical view of what Dr. M Schonerts should look like.

Mathilde, or more accurately her Zimmer frame, navigates a course between stacks of books and papers, leading us into her side office. Mathilde lowers herself into her desk chair and switches on the computer. The room is cluttered and airless. People have far more to say about Mathilde's poor housekeeping and unkempt appearance than her scientific brilliance. If Mathilde was a man, it would be all smiles and proclamations of, "He's an eccentric genius" and women in his orbit running around clearing up after him.

I hate gender stereotyping. "There's no doubt that Mathilde is a genius! Give her some slack! Let her work!" I yelled at a gossiping secretary just before the summer break. I know all about being a woman in a man's world. It began when I was the only girl in my Physics A-level class. It was back in the 1980s, a time when it wasn't the teacher's job to sort out squabbles and disputes. Every week, for a year and a half, the boys had dismantled my experiments. Dr. Stevenson, in his tweed jacket and bow tie, seemed oblivious to the class antics. One day, Andy Waterhouse, over six-foot tall and rugby captain, upped the ante after messing with my experiment; he gave me a Chinese burn. I hit back. I kneed him in the nuts causing him to fall to the floor in agony. Dr. Stevenson turned to see what the commotion was about and laughed at Andy. After that none of the boys ever went near my experiments again.

None of this would have happened if I'd been at the local all-girls school. Mrs. Winn, our neighbour, who was secretary at Edgbaston High School for Girls, told us, "This year there are more girls doing science than humanities A-Levels. Isn't it wonderful!" Sadly my parents, although not poor, couldn't afford the fees at the time.

Charlie initiates a few moments of chit-chat.

"How are the holidays going?" he asks. I'm not quite sure why, when we have so many more interesting things to discuss. Maybe Charlie is just being nosy.

"How did Nav's A-levels go?" asks Mathilde.

"Five A*s," I say proudly.

"Always a bright one. I could do with him here," chuckles Mathilde. "An off-the-record internship."

I consider it. Nav could work with Mathilde, put his knowledge to good use, rather than being stuck in that dingy repair shop.

Luckily, we soon leave the topic of family and get on to mathematics and science.

"The team haven't crunched the numbers yet. There isn't anything I can tell you about nature versus nurture and intelligence per se," explains Mathilde.

Oh, then why am I here? I think. *Have I got a 99.9% chance of some terrible genetic illness? Why on earth did I offer up my unique DNA for such close scrutiny?* I know the answer: for science and because of Mathilde. I can trust Mathilde. We both share a dislike of campus gossip.

Charlie looks on earnestly. It will be his job to collate everyone's data ready for Mathilde to review. "Will you be checking this?"

"Sure," I say. I am happy to check Mathilde's work as there won't be much to ratify. I know she will look at the evidence as if it's an unbreakable code. Day and night she will live and breathe the results. Hopefully before her contract is up and she has to return to Belgium, she will see something obvious and groundbreaking. If I'm really honest, I would love to be part of that team.

I hope Mathilde's contract will be extended, and my favourite colleague will be allowed to stay longer in the UK. But I've heard rumours in the office about how foreign staff are struggling to get work visas. After Brexit, collaboration with European scientists will become more and more difficult. It saddens me that Mathilde's days here are probably numbered—and there's nothing I can do about it.

"This is a courtesy meeting, we invite all our volunteers to a one-to-one," continues Mathilde in her professional persona. "And to ask you to sign the final disclaimers." She pushes the papers and a pen across the desk.

I speed read and sign.

"Although there is no payment involved, we can offer you some information in exchange for your time. We can give you a printout of medical likelihoods and predispositions."

Is this why I'm here? A shiver runs down my spine. "No thank you," I say flatly. "I don't want to know anything medical. You do what you want with that data."

"What about your ethnicity?" asks Mathilde. "Sorry if I sound like I'm trying to sell you car insurance." She laughs lightly.

Charlie raises his eyebrows. It's been a while since Mathilde has revealed her sense of humour. Our eyes meet and Charlie and I smile fondly.

"Ethnicity?" I ask with cautious interest.

"The whole DNA ethnicity thing has become a bit of a white person's game. We can pinpoint which part of England Charlie's descendants come from."

"Yorkshire and the Isle of Man. Plus three per cent Greek!" says Charlie with a shrug.

"And my long line of Flemish ancestors plus ten per cent Western Swedish. But for those of Asian and African heritage, the data is very general. Patchy."

"Why?" I ask.

"Quite simple, really. Not as many people from those areas take DNA tests in the first place," says Mathilde staring intently at the screen. "Anyway, in the end we will see that everyone in the world is mixed-race. We all have many ancestors. Many identities to celebrate. The end to war and to ethnic cleansing." She presses print.

Charlie gallantly fetches the printout and hands it to me. A pie chart! "I like it. At the end of the day, I have been turned into a simple primary school pie chart of colourful wedges!"

"What did you expect, hey?" says Mathilde.

"On the ethnicity or graph style?"

"Ethnicity, of course!"

"Well I expected to be South Asian, and I am," I look down at the paper again. "Ninety-two per cent South Asian to be exact. But the two per cent Baltic and six per cent Scottish must be from the Empire days." I smile.

"Every human being is mixed-race. It is an essential ingredient of being human. Do you want to look for matches? It's unlikely that there will be close matches, but you never know. Many people will find some very distant cousins," explains Mathilde.

"I have too many cousins already!" I say.

"You never know what relatives are out there. Those *you* don't even know about!" laughs Mathilde scrolling down the screen. "Family secrets." She leans forward and peers into the computer screen.

It's then that a usually suppressed memory from a difficult time before I even met Maneer comes into my mind. Over the years I'd blocked out feelings of loss and grief; taken on board the British "stiff upper lip". My brother, Nabeel, and I have been the guardians of a family secret which at times has taken its toll. A few years back, with the advancement of the internet, Google, Facebook and Friends Reunited, my curiosity had grown and I'd made some searches. But all my hopes came to nothing. Then, after reading a whole series of detective novels, I toyed with the idea of hiring a private investigator. But I had so little to go on. There were rumours of course, but rumours aren't facts. The investigator would probably want to speak to Maneer, and I couldn't bear the thought of dragging him into it all. He'd never think of my family in the same way again. I had put the memory back in to the far reaches of my mind again until this very moment.

"Are you okay, Maryam?" asks Charlie.

"I'm fine," I reply coming out of my trance-like state.

"Ah," says Mathilde, "There is this: a mixed profile linked to yours…which is a bit unexpected knowing your family."

What does she mean by knowing my family? Mathilde had been one of the few colleagues who'd been over to the house for barbeques and other meals. The woman lives alone in a riverside apartment, and I was brought up to see mealtimes as a communal event. And it was always an opportunity for Nav and Mathilde to chat, which I liked to encourage.

"I'll print it off," says Mathilde.

Nav

Norwich City is playing at home today. It's 3pm and the football match has just kicked off. This means a quiet afternoon in the shop. With almost no customers and all the repairs done, my thoughts keep returning to Lucie. I want to speak to her, to continue our conversation about family trees and how best to represent that sort of data when she gets the match results.

I download a family tree DNA app. I test drive it with my own family. I fill in my parent's full dates of birth. Places of birth: Birmingham and Manchester respectively. I move the Nav icon around unsure whether I should be at the top or bottom of this chart. I add aunts, uncles, cousins. Soon enough there's a whole load of details I can't fill in. I don't know my grandparents' dates of birth. There's no way they'd tell me, either!

I fiddle with the app moving my family around like chess pieces in an online game. Except this game has limited options. It won't let me have the same cousin descended from both my great-grandparents. I have cousins in the States who I am distantly related to through both my mum and my dad's family. No one has thought to programme an app for the extended and extensive Asian family! We don't follow the UK average of 1.7 children in our family, and therefore have many more cousins than the average British citizen. Would a Venn diagram work better? I search for somewhere to send the company my suggestion.

Maybe I should take a DNA test? A while back, over dinner, Mum was going on about the DNAcademia project at the university. "Is our intelligence inherently linked to our genes?" she asked.

"Not the nature versus nurture debate again," said Dad.

"What's that?" asked Nadiya.

"In psychological terms it is the extent to which particular aspects of intelligence and behaviour are a product of inheritance or learned characteristics," said Mum.

"What?" asked Nadiya, clearly confused.

"For example; is Nav good at maths because it's in his genes or because we sent him to study sessions and gave him revision books for his birthday?" asks Dad.

Nadiya looked at me expectantly. I shrugged.

Dad added that offering the "carrot" of ethnicity and relative matches in exchange for freely taking an IQ test and giving away raw data wasn't wholly ethical.

Mum said that was just another way to check on the findings, and added, "Nav would make a good candidate."

"Stop talking about our son as if he's *not in the room*," said Dad, completely unaware that he'd just done the same!

"Mum, why not me? Why can't I do the tests?" moaned Nadiya. "Is it because I'm a girl?"

"No, Nadiya. This is nothing to do with gender. The results of genetic testing can be a lot to take in. Knowledge about our genes can be life changing," said Dad, getting up from the table and leaving his dinner half eaten.

"What about me?" chipped in Muni, looking down at his trousers. "How can all these things be in my jeans?"

Nadiya fell about laughing.

I think about Lucie and how genetic testing is changing her life. Dad wouldn't have to know if I took a test. There may be some surprises, things I could tell Lucie about. If I go back a few generations, I might have some English or Scottish blood in me. After all, the British were in India for nearly a hundred years until independence in 1947. I've never thought much about my past, our family history.

History lessons at school were always about other people's histories. The Tudor kings and queens, Victorians and the industrial revolution, the suffragettes, dictators and World Wars—all events which none of my ancestors had anything to do with—became my story. I never felt excluded. The lessons didn't feel strange—this was history on the default setting.

When I got home, I told Dad. He said, "Ah, but we fought on the Turks' side in World War One, and then there were many, many soldiers from the Indian subcontinent who fought in World War Two." I didn't know whether to quite believe him and walked off. At college it wasn't until Black History month that anyone mentioned the British Empire from my ancestors' point of view. And it felt very odd. History is usually told from the victor's point of view.

Back to the family tree app. I need my grandparents' dates of birth. I'll slip next door and ask Uncle Nabeel.

Nabeel

I am in the middle of negotiations with the double-glazing company when Nav wafts in waving around his phone, going on about who goes where on the family tree. I hold my hand up and hope he gets the message to shut up. "You are behind schedule and if you don't get more workers back here on Monday, you'll owe me a delay payment!" I bark down the phone.

Nav jumps nervously on hearing my businessman voice. "The ball is in your court," I say ending the call.

"So what can I do for my favourite nephew?" I ask.

"I need everyone in the family's date of birth. I'm making a family tree," he says with that naïve smile of his. I do worry about the boy. He is so unworldly wise. I was working shifts at McDonald's and taking on the family business at his age. He reminds me of… *Don't think it! And absolutely don't say it! I tell myself. Don't give anything away beyond the place and year of your parent's birth!* I'm not into all this digging up the past. Not now, after all these years.

Today the boy's asking for dates of birth. What next? Searching for birth, death and marriage certificates? Census results? That boy is too bright for his own good. And more importantly where will it lead a clever boy like him? Nav believes in knowledge for knowledge's sake. All that time he spends studying, rather like my dear sister Maryam.

"No problem," I say as lightly as possible, concealing my unease. Everything is connected. I know this only too well from my business dealings. If push comes to shove, I will find a way to put a stop to all this digging up the past. *Someone in the family has to do the right thing. That's what I did before. And I'm prepared to act this time too.*

Sunday 21ˢᵗ August

Lucie

I pass Mum on the landing. She's carrying a tray in the direction of Maisie's bedroom. The build-up to my sister's GCSE results begins. There's already an atmosphere in the house. I don't mean being nasty to each other or anything like that. More like an unspoken expectation of being unbelievably nice to Maisie.

I eye up the mouth-watering plate of poached eggs on toast and a tall glass of orange juice with juicy bits. "Is that for me?" I ask, knowing full well it's for Maisie.

"Shush, I'm not sure if she's awake yet," says Mum.

"Well, if she's not going to wake up when you take that in, I'll eat it then!" I say. "It won't be nice cold." I never get breakfast in bed.

Mum smiles weakly. "It's so gloomy outside. The sort of day to sleep in," she says looking at the rain still hammering on the window.

I've had enough of it already: walking around on eggshells to avert Maisie going into a meltdown. If only they knew how *I* feel! Imagine waiting to find out precisely where in the world your real biological father is from. To find out if you have brothers, sisters, aunts, uncles that you never knew about! I'm not the result of some immaculate conception. I am not Jesus Christ. Nor do I want to be! I want to be human. Normal. Like everyone else. That has to be a much bigger event than GCSE results anxiety syndrome. They don't come out until Thursday anyway. Usually, I feel guilty when I get narked about Mum's special treatment of Maisie—she's always struggled at school (she and Dad are dyslexic). But today I can't help thinking: *Just another thing that shows she's related to him and I'm not.*

To be honest I don't really feel anxious about the results which will pinpoint where in South Asia my father is from. The years of not knowing anything at all about my biological father were what sometimes drove me crazy.

The rain's never going to stop, and I don't know what to do today. I'd give anything to get out of the house, away from Mum, Dad and Maisie. But it's Sunday, which means no buses until first thing tomorrow. I could walk. That would be the only way of getting out of the village before Monday. If the rain wasn't lashing down, I'd consider walking the six miles into town. I feel like a prisoner in my own home. How I wish I'd taken up Mum and Dad's offer of driving lessons.

I go back and hide out in my bedroom. Sunday. "Nothing day" would be a better description of today. Dad's gone to fix someone's burst pipe. Mum is working on her laptop. I could binge watch a series on Netflix—but I don't really want to do that. I feel restless. Trapped. A horrible not knowing what to do with myself feeling. I need to talk to someone. I grab my phone from the bedside table and send Nav a message.

Lucie: Hey

Nav: Hey

Lucie: Any news? Results?

Nav: Sorry. Not yet. Not a good day.

Lucie: What's up?

Nav: Hiding in my room. Nephews and nieces have cabin fever. They've got it bad.

Lucie: Agh…The rain?

Nav: Yes! Rainy Sundays!

Lucie: Is it statistically more likely to rain on a Sunday?

Nav: No! Of course not!

Lucie: Just joking.

Nav: A heatwave is on its way.

Lucie: Really?

A link arrives from Nav. A meteorological forecast with an amber weather warning. It says the weather will hit 32 degrees Celsius by Thursday.

> Lucie: We have to wait it out. We're transitioning. Liminal like the weather.

I like using the word liminal. I learnt it in English Literature. Neither one state nor another. From the Latin word limen, meaning threshold. Standing at the threshold. It pretty much sums me *and* the weather up, as does the term pathetic fallacy.

I send Nav a link to pathetic fallacy in literature.

> Nav: Got to go. Kids are banging on my door—again!

Are they really banging on his door, or have I been too deep and meaningful? But no, I think as he's super smart he will be interested.

I message Jenny. I have no idea when my stream of messages, which seem like a one-sided conversation, will arrive in her feed. She's only on holiday in France for a few weeks but it seems like forever. And I have to tell someone. I tell her about my South Asian DNA. I tell her about Nav helping me in my search. Last summer when she was in Turkey, she said she saw so many people who looked just like me. And, as if she needed any further proof, I ate all the pistachio Turkish Delight she brought back as a present in one go. "Luce, you *must* be part Turkish," said Jenny.

Nav

More banging on my bedroom door. I ignore it for a bit. The kids keep it up as if this is the best game ever. I go to the door again. I'm about to yell at them, or chase them down the hall, but come face to face with Mum.

"The rain has just about stopped. Can you take your cousins to the park?"

"Why does everyone assume I should be the one to take them to the park? As if I don't have anything better to do. Or need any privacy. Nadiya should deal with them. Not because she's a girl, or the next eldest, but because she's the bossiest." I don't actually say any of this. Nor do I say, "I want to sit in my room and reply to Lucie." I compose a message right now saying: *Yes, I get what you mean by liminal. In science liminal is used to describe some transitional phases.*

I have so much more to write but instead, I say "Sure, Mum."

"Thanks. Nadiya's had enough of them and taken to her bed! I almost forget sometimes that she's a teenager!"

So instead of discussing liminality from the sanctuary of my bedroom I follow Mum downstairs into the mayhem of the utility room and supervise the putting on of wellies. There's no way I'm wearing wellies to go beyond the garden. They're for little kids and old people. I tie up my trainers.

Dad is cooking Sunday lunch and chatting to Aunty Mona. Wafts of roast lamb seasoned with cumin make their way from the kitchen into the utility room. I'm starving. I forgot all about breakfast. I steal into the kitchen and grab a banana from the fruit bowl.

"Nav, you're a good boy, taking your cousins out," says Aunty Mona.

"Anything for you, Aunty Mona," I say with a cheesy smile. I'm also about to remind her I'm no longer a boy but a young man now, but before I can say anything my little cousin, Anmar, grabs our attention. He is running around in circles like a frustrated puppy.

"What's up, mate?" I ask.

"My anorak is gone!" he screams.

"Where did you leave it?" replies Aunty Mona.

There's a great commotion and I wait whilst the adults run around the house in search of Anmar's anorak.

"Under the sofa," says Uncle Nabeel handing it over.

I finally take the kids outside. They throw themselves down the path like caged animals being set free. I set a timer on my phone and tell them they have half an hour at the park. There's nowhere dry to sit so I loiter around unsure what to do. Surprisingly Muni doesn't mind racing around the wet play equipment with his little cousins. Eventually I call time and shepherd them back to the house. Once they're in the front garden I head round to the back. I need some child-free time!

I contemplate hiding out in the summer house, when through the French windows I spy Mum and Uncle Nabeel huddled together at one end of the dining room table. From their strained expressions they are probably discussing, or more likely disagreeing about, the big student housing contract. I don't understand her problem with it, with him moving some of the business from Birmingham into Norfolk.

Dad and Aunty Mona walk in on them. Mum and Uncle Nabeel stop talking and smile inanely at each other. Uncle Nabeel never likes to discuss business when Dad's around. That's what they always say. Or is Lucie right in thinking there is something shifty and secretive about Uncle Nabeel? I've never noticed that before.

I make my way across the patio and go in through the French window.

"Nav! Take your shoes off!" yells Mum. "Look at the mud on my floorboards!"

Dad and Uncle Nabeel look on, grinning at me in an all-men-together sympathetic way.

Mum glares at me. "Sorry," I mumble. Obediently I sit down on the floor and unlace my trainers.

The four of them chat for a bit.

"Leila's not joining us for lunch?" says Aunty Mona. I like Uncle Nabeel's wife, but she hardly ever comes to visit.

Uncle Nabeel shakes his head. "She's a home bird."

"I would be too, if I lived in a house as grand as yours," says Aunty Mona. That's not what Aunty Mona says behind his back. She calls Aunty Leila a caged bird.

"It's a long trip from Birmingham for lunch. And she wouldn't want to camp out on-site like me!"

"Leila is always welcome to stay here," says Mum. "As are you, Nabeel."

"I like to stay in my properties. See it from the users' point of view. Best way to iron out any building niggles."

I panic and wonder if Uncle Nabeel is going to say something about me and Lucie visiting him. Sometimes my parents are too interested in our friends. At seventeen I deserve some privacy. I don't want to attract any attention, so decide it's best just to hide out behind the sofa until they've all gone.

"I'll go and check on lunch," says Dad looking uncomfortable and heading out.

"Let me help," says Aunty Mona trailing after her big brother. It reminds me of how Nadiya used to follow me around—until she started high school, then she wanted nothing to do with me.

"Why are you doing this?" hisses Uncle Nabeel. "Opening things up after all this time. I have a public profile."

What things? They've forgotten I'm here!

"Same old story: it's always business before family with you," whispers Mum.

"Same old story: it's always you taking the moral high ground; me having to bail everyone out," says Uncle Nabeel storming off.

What was that about? There are footsteps across the floor and the slam of the door. Mum and Uncle Nabeel have gone. Phew! I'm finally alone. I'm intrigued, but also quite used to their bickering. I'm not going to get another moment to myself until Aunty Mona and her kids leave on Wednesday evening, when she takes Nadiya and Mani back with her again for a few days. I take my phone out of my jeans pocket.

Nav: Are you free on Thursday?

Lucie: Sure.

The reply comes almost immediately. It seems she isn't annoyed that I've taken so long to get back to her. Everything is okay. I pick up my soggy trainers, slip back into the hall and place them in the shoe rack. I message Archie and see if he's up for playing a bit of online chess.

Tuesday 23ʳᵈ August

Lucie

I don't know where yesterday went. It's like that some days in the summer holidays they just go by with nothing happening. Tuesday is a blue day. A pale blue day. Not powder blue, or even cobalt. It's a duller, sugar paper kind of blue.

"Urgh, why does Tuesday have to be so blue?" I complain to Maisie, but she misunderstands me completely.

"I know, I'm *so* blue," she tells me. "I can't stand waiting for these GCSE results. And once I get them everyone's going to be so weirdly nice but disappointed at me." She looks at me. "Wait, why are you blue?"

"I'm not," I say. "Tuesday is, you know like Monday is a sort of navy blue, and Wednesday is bottle-green. Then orange and red come at the end of the week."

Maisie looks at me like I've just sprouted an extra head. "Is this some kind of artist thing, or should I be worried about you?" she asks.

I'm not in the mood to explain myself. "Some kind of artist thing," I agree.

I feel like Nav would understand. I wonder if Tuesday is blue for him too? I could message him and ask. I'm sure this is a normal thing. Google will know though.

I flop on the sofa and scroll looking for links between colour and days of the week and discover something called Synaesthesia, a neurological condition in which two or more senses are linked. Apparently, the excitement of one sense stimulates the experience of the other. The website explains that someone with synaesthesia might perceive certain letters and numbers simultaneously as colours. It also says that synaesthesia develops in childhood when children are engaged in abstract concepts for the first time.

I'd love to know what Nav has to say about this, but it seems too complicated to write about in a text message. The thing is, it is so boring here that I just want to go to art school right now, where I have people to talk to about all my ideas and a big studio to paint and draw in. All I seem to do is waste time scrolling through my phone waiting for something interesting to happen. There is nothing to do here at home, alone in the middle of nowhere. I even went for a walk round the estate but ended up wishing we had a dog so I wouldn't look like I didn't have any friends! Aren't people supposed to enjoy their summer holidays? Mum is always saying, "Thank God it's the end of term and the holidays are here." Dad is always counting down the days until he has one of his rare days off. Why? I just want to be somewhere else. I want to see Nav and chat about things no one at home would understand. Thursday, when—fingers crossed—my results will be in, is a whole two days away. Jenny is *still* in France. And Sam and

Josephine—my only real college friends—have jobs. I'm in limbo. I want to be in London and be an art student now—not next month! I suppose I could work on my project for university and pretend I'm there already.

I hunt around the bedroom for my new sketchbook. It was a present from Mum. Well, not exactly a present, as she has a whole stack of them at work for her photography students. Other people's parents bring home biros and envelopes. Mum brings sketchbooks. Dad brings bits of pipe work, which I used for my postmodernist sculpture project. Maisie helped me build my own version of the Pompidou Centre in Paris with bits of piping slotted together to construct the exterior. After we'd painted it blue and silver it looked pretty much like the real thing—albeit in miniature!

There it is, the brand-new sketchbook poking out from under my bed. I peel off the plastic wrapper and open the first page. It's an exciting moment, when you're confronted with a whole book of clean white pages. A blank canvas of endless possibilities. I take out a pack of coloured pencils and arrange them on my desk. My summer holiday task is to create a surface pattern design; a repeat image for wallpaper, fabric or gift-wrap which says something about me, my identity and what's important to me. I know the key colour for starters: turquoise. It has been my favourite colour since I was about ten. Before that I always loved yellow. Unlike Maisie, I never went through a pink phase, which she's only just emerging from.

I open the window and peer out across the fields seeking inspiration. If the task was to paint a picture which says something about me, the golden fields against a blue sky could look pretty dramatic. I could paint a swirly sky and use vertical brush marks like in Van Gogh's *Wheat Field*. But it is just the same old view I've seen for most of my life and it doesn't interest me. I breathe in the still, humid air. There isn't even a hint of a breeze. What shapes? What patterns? Back at my desk I doodle. I sketch circular and spiral shapes in golden orange—I tell myself it's an abstracted version of hay bales. Then I let my imagination run riot and the circles become onion domes and the background a contrasting burgundy and purple.

I wonder where these shapes and colours are coming from? Maybe they represent my inner life, all those things swirling around in my dreams and subconscious? I have to write notes alongside the design. What do I see? Is this like the ink blot test? Beauty or ugliness in the eye of the beholder? I used to do this when I was a kid. I saw all kinds of things in my old bedroom curtains. Flowers became fairies and leaves turned into witches.

I gaze into the colours and patterns. I see my South Asian heritage. Is it just me that can see this? What would Nav see? We learnt all about our subconscious when we studied Dada and Surrealism—which was all about our dream world. Natalie, my art tutor, said the automatic writing and drawing was like the ink blot test where Rorschach explored his subjects' perceptions of ink blots and recorded and analysed them using psychological interpretations, complex algorithms or both. Until I met Nav I never thought much about maths and art. They are such an unlikely combination, much like our new friendship.

I remember how university professors like to see the research, so I write about how some psychologists use this test to examine an individual's personal characteristics and emotional functioning.

The Rorschach test is projective, the idea being that when a person is shown an ambiguous, meaningless image, their mind will work hard to find meaning. I make my designs more abstract, to match my complicated family history. Perhaps this is why people get all hung up about abstract art, because like the ink blot test, their mind wants to find meaning? Why can't some people appreciate lines, shapes, colours and patterns without interpretation and meaning?

Nav

I can't believe there is still another two days until Aunty Mona and her kids return to Manchester. This summer, life is impossible with them here. I can't believe I used to like them coming to stay!

The problem is, my own brother and sister's personalities change when their cousins are staying. Nadiya becomes bossier, and Muni starts acting like he is the age of Mona's kids, which means spending most of the time rolling around on the floor with Anmar. Secondly, no one seems to notice that I can no longer live the life of a normal seventeen-year-old. I'm itching to start my new life away from the mayhem of home. What's more, today I can't wait to see Lucie and talk about interesting things. Nor can I wait to be in Cambridge, living alongside people my own age who want to talk about science, like, how do you determine the spin state of an electron? Even Mum doesn't want to talk quantum physics. She also seems distracted by the chaos at home.

Everyone talks about boring, mundane things. Like at the weekend when the whole house was on red alert hunting down Anmar's anorak. Even simple pleasures like listening to music, or watching a YouTube tutorial (or even necessities like taking a quick pee!) are impossible. One of them is always banging on the door looking for me.

Thank God there's one last vestige of privacy: inside my head. They can't barge in on me there. If they did, they'd get a surprise: so many thoughts of our family and about Lucie's DNA test results.

When I think about Lucie, I realise I shouldn't be so annoyed about having such a big extended family. But there does always seem to be too much family, and when they visit, they stay so much longer than Archie's cousins or grandparents.

I also keep thinking about how I've always taken my heritage for granted. We may live across three continents, but we can all trace our heritage on Mum's side back to Gojra in Pakistan. I keep wondering what it must mean for Lucie not knowing anything about her father, grandparents, or cousins.

I know my identity in that sense. She's never had that security. She's had no one, until me, to talk to about race and what it means to be brown skinned in a very white town. That means a lot to me, but it makes our friendship really special for Lucie.

Wednesday 24th August

Lucie

Up here in the treehouse I get a bird's eye view of a silhouette emerging from the house. Dad's making a run for it in the direction of the shed. Even he's been driven out of the house by Mum's cleaning frenzy. She claims it is too hot to clean during the day.

"No, Mais. Not like that! Wrap them around the ledge!" I say.

"What are you two doing up there in the dark?" calls Dad.

"There's nowhere else to escape to," is what I want to say.

Maisie gets in first. "We're testing out Lucie's fairy lights. They've been out in the garden charging up all day."

I wrap the end of the lead and the last couple of stars around the ladder and switch them on.

"Wow! They're so cool," says Maisie.

Dad stands at the bottom of the ladder. He gives a thumbs up. "I'll tell your nan they were a success," he says heading into the shed.

The solar powered lights along with the envelope of cash were birthday presents from Nana Pat. She always gives the best presents. Sometimes I wish she was my biological nana.

Mum's mum, Muriel, died when I was a baby. I only know her through old photos of a pale prim woman with short, stiff hair. This forces me to wonder about my biological father's mother. Is there a grandmother alive and well somewhere miles away from here that I've never met?

Maisie makes herself comfortable by shuffling onto a cushion and wrapping a tartan blanket around herself, even though it's warm enough to be outside in just a T-shirt. Her legs are wrapped across mine; we've always had a close sisterly bond. I still don't have the heart to tell her about all the thoughts whirring around in my head, however. I wouldn't know where to begin.

"I love it up here," says Maisie. "All the twinkling lights make it look like a festival. Remember that year Mum and Dad took us to Latitude and the lake was lit up?"

"I do. That seems so long ago."

Maisie sighs. "It's a bit of a relief to have our own space. Is it just me, or do you think it's a bit much having Mum *and* Dad around most of the time in the summer—at our age? Don't people need their kitchens and bathrooms fixed in the school holidays?"

"Customers are away on holiday, I guess."

"Don't you just wish they both had normal nine-to-five jobs? Then we'd know in advance when they're around, and going to be invading our personal space."

"Yes, I do." I open some Bourbon biscuits—the only thing other than packets of pasta and rice that were left in the kitchen cupboard. I pass one to Maisie. "At least Mum goes into the art school occasionally over the summer."

"Yeah, thank God!" says Maisie her mouth full of biscuit. "It would be good if we could have the house to ourselves for a whole weekend, though."

"We could send them on holiday so we can have a party?" I say pulling the blanket over me.

"If they went away for a weekend, we could blast my music really loud and even have a mini festival!"

"The neighbours would love that," I say sarcastically. I break the biscuit in two and eat the buttercream half.

"Why do you always do that?" says Maisie, copying my biscuit manoeuvre.

"Because I'm the clever one," I say.

"What?"

"The pleasure of eating the biscuit lasts a whole lot longer." There's an awkward silence. I break another biscuit into two and wonder what to say next. "How are you feeling about getting your results tomorrow?" I ask.

"I don't care about my results," says Maisie.

She's lying. Everyone cares about their results, one way or another.

"One thing is for sure. I'm going out with the gang afterward to commiserate or celebrate. Luce, you take after Mum, passing exams and all that. I'm practical. I like talking to people. Socialising is my hobby. I'm the one who takes after Dad."

"Why would I take after Dad? It's not like he's my *real* dad!" I tell her.

"I forget. I mean he *is* your dad though, *really*. Don't you think? He does all the dad stuff."

"He *is* and *isn't*. I mean look at me! Do you think I look like him?"

"No," sighs Maisie.

"When I was little Mum told me all kinds of different things about my *real* father. Once she said I was an IVF baby. Another time she said I was a miracle baby. Mostly she said I was fathered by a sperm donor, because she was a feminist and wanted a child without a man in tow."

"If she's such a feminist, why did she change her name from Kitchener to Hansen?" asks Maisie.

"No idea. What I do know is, Mum *not* talking about my biological father gets on my nerves."

Maisie screws up her pretty freckled face in sympathy. So many times, when I was little, I wished I looked like Maisie. I wished I had a face which fitted in around here, like Maisie's does. All the heroines in our favourite childhood books, the classics which everyone knows, look like Maisie. Lola, from *Charlie and Lola* and all the children in *We're Going on a Bear Hunt* to name a few. And where are the girls who look like me in Harry Potter? At least the Disney princesses have Pocahontas and Princess Jasmine. And Maisie has Cinderella and Sleeping Beauty who look like her. There definitely needs to be more female leads with Asian heritage in children's books.

"Maybe your dad was a one-night stand and she's too embarrassed to admit it amongst the great and good of the village? Or there were a few men on the scene and she didn't know which one it was?" she suggests eventually.

"That's gross!"

"It's not that bad. It's like in *Mamma Mia* when Sophie doesn't know which of Donna's exes is her father. Mum loved that film. She cried in the cinema, which is *so* unlike her."

"That doesn't mean she *is* Donna! I hope you didn't make ungrounded assumptions like this in your English Literature exam," I suddenly realise that I've overreacted. "I'm so sorry. I shouldn't have said that."

"Can I say a thing *you* might not like?" asks Maisie.

"What do you want to say?" I'm intrigued.

"Well, if Mum had IVF, or a sperm donor or whatever," Maisie pauses. "Don't you think she'd have chosen a father who looked more…"

Silence.

"Like her," I say breaking the tension.

Maisie hides her face under the cover. A muffled, "I'm not being racist," seeps through the blanket.

"Multicultural stuff is pretty popular now with festivals and food markets. But Mum has always been into it, hasn't she?" I say.

"I know. But why would she deliberately make someone's life harder."

"Maisie! That's an awful thing to say." I'm glad I can't see her face. Why does Maisie always have to put into words the things that you're not supposed to say?

"I don't agree with it!" shouts Maisie popping her head out for air. "It's how the world is. I wish the world wasn't like that. I wish that all women earned the same as men; I wish top jobs didn't go to the same old white men who went to private schools."

"I know, it's a crap way to run the world," I mutter.

"Mum knows all that. And when we went to Paris with the school it was only Ranjit and Mr. Yassin who got stopped by the customs officers. They've both got British passports and were born here. They're treated differently because of the colour of their skin," says Maisie, desperate to prove her point in the debate.

"And because of their name, too," I add.

"But then Mr. Yassin announced he wouldn't be going on the New York trip."

"I get that. But nor did you. It was too expensive!"

"Only the really rich kids went," huffs Maisie.

"There were some people at college who'd never been abroad. There were even two girls in my art class who'd never been to London."

"I do understand that we are privileged. But what I wish most..." says Maisie, her voice almost a whisper, "Is that I wasn't dyslexic and have to stay on at the end of exams for *extra time* when everyone else gets to go home. I'll still do worse than all those who got to leave before me."

"It's scary being different." I never guessed Maisie thought about these things. Things which aren't to do with boys, or how she looks. I've massively underestimated her.

Before I know it, I tell my sister all about the phone saga, the DNA test and Nav helping me. My face is burning and for once Maisie is quiet. I feel so relieved to finally be getting this off my chest.

"Your father could be from so many places," says Maisie.

Talking to Maisie makes my head race with so many possibilities. Who is my father? What is his name? Where exactly is he from? Delhi? Mumbai? Kabul? Colombo? Kathmandu? What is his profession? A professor? A plumber? An artist? A pauper? A homeless person? A millionaire? Everything and anything is possible.

Did my mother meet him? Was he some one-night stand like Maisie said? Maybe he was the love of my mother's life? Or possibly a holiday romance? I wonder if Steve knows about any of this? Every time I think of a question, it just throws up more questions and uncertainties.

"Don't tell Mum and Dad any of this. You're sworn to secrecy."

"Sure. I can keep a secret," says Maisie. My heart's pounding. Should I really have told her?

Tori

Cleaning is a welcome distraction, an exercise in mindfulness, I tell myself. I'm worried about my daughters and as I scrub and polish I try and think what to do. Maybe I'm overreacting and the air of tension in the house is all perfectly normal. A-level results, followed by GCSE results a week later would do the same to any household. Except that the odd atmosphere began before then, something changed around the time of Lucie's eighteenth birthday. That's when I started to notice Lucie distancing herself more, staying out later with friends and, when she was home, staying in her room all alone. But there's no tangible reason why, nothing that I can put my finger on. Perhaps she is simply growing up now that she is getting ready to move to London for university, but I can't help but feel a distance has grown between us over the last few weeks.

I also can't help but think that it is my fault. Is this all to do with the fact that I'd told myself that when Lucie turned eighteen, I'd tell her everything I knew about her biological father? Tell her the whole story of her origins, or as much of it that I could bare to discuss. Lucie's eighteenth birthday came and went by so quickly, and I couldn't face the truth. Then at the book club I promised myself that I'd tell her.

Back in the late nineties when Lucie was born the world felt a different place. The world seemed more hopeful and tolerant. Since the Berlin Wall had fallen in 1989, Europe had felt more welcoming to outsiders. To me it seemed like the mood of acceptance and celebration of diversity went right on up until the London Olympics in 2012. It scares me how much the world has changed recently—everybody so polarised in their opinions—and what that may mean for Lucie.

The world of politics has put an end, or hopefully just a pause, to all that acceptance. Even Pat, my mother-in-law, who relies increasingly on the Portuguese district nurse, says she doesn't want immigrants here. I want to challenge her and ask where that left Lucie, her granddaughter. But that would have meant opening up a whole can of worms that I hadn't even told Lucie, let alone Steve's mother, about.

Since Lucie's birthday, I have waited and hoped for another chance to have the talk with Lucie. I almost told her the day I dropped her in the city to collect her phone, but Lucie seemed distracted, so I let the moment pass. I knew she didn't really want to be seen out in town with her mother. I understood. I was the same at that age. Then in my twenties

I did the thing I never dreamed of: I found myself living back at home with my own mother, with a baby in tow. It just happened that way. My mother and I found ourselves grief stricken. Mum mourning the loss of her husband of many years, and me—always a bit of a Daddy's girl—mourning the loss of my father.

*

But that is jumping ahead. I do remember being Lucie's age. I stayed living at home for a year whilst doing my Art Foundation course at Colchester Institute, while my school friends moved away for their degree courses. I finally got to leave home for Art School, The London College of Printing, where I studied photography and graphic design. By my second year I'd spent less and less time travelling back to Essex to see my parents. They were always so busy with their friends, golf, mini-breaks, and cheese and wine evenings to find a space in the diary for me—their only daughter. My father was still working then, doing the daily commute, every day for forty years to Liverpool Street station and a brisk walk to his office. I'd occasionally met him for lunch, and more often than not brought a hungry friend along for pie and mash too. I still have the photographs of Leadenhall Market with stall holders displaying their wares. Huge carcasses strung up against the tiled columns of the elegant Victorian arcade. The black and white pictures formed part of my degree show. I sold them to a lifestyle magazine which helped to pay for my round-the-world flight ticket.

I returned to the UK to find that after my father's retirement, they'd sold up and moved to rural Norfolk. The first I heard of it was a letter I received at the Post Restante in New Delhi.

I moved back to London, into a flat in Streatham and touted my photography portfolio around art directors' offices. I worked freelance for a number of publications back when print was king and cutting-edge design was to be found on the covers and inside pages of music and fashion magazines.

One sunny summer weekend I visited my parents in the country. I photographed the yellow rapeseed fields set against a big blue sky. I promised to return soon, but was so busy with commissions and getting my career going, that my second visit to their rural idyll, the well-kept bungalow with a view, was later than I'd hoped for.

In 1997 I returned to the small village again shortly before Christmas. The funeral service for my father was held in St Mary's church, with its quintessential thatched roof and round tower built from flint. A timeless place where I have since attended numerous school harvest festivals and carol services.

Looking back, I'm unsure if the feelings of nausea at my father's funeral were because of my pregnancy, or the shock of my father's sudden death. The icy cold church was packed. The car park overflowed with family, friends and former colleagues. He was the first of their generation to die. A heart attack in his sleep. "Quick and painless," everyone said, as if that was any consolation.

My mother fell to pieces. As the only child, it fell upon me to spend my free time travelling up to Norfolk. I never dreamt that in eighteen months' time I'd be back in the same church, with baby Lucie, for my mother's funeral. Sometimes I wonder if my mother died of a broken heart. Or was it disappointment in her husband and daughter's failure to live up to her high standards? I received my parents' property in her will and so I stayed. A fresh start.

*

As I polish the bathroom taps, I am reminded of my mother, probably the last generation of women expected to stay at home and be a housewife. She was a fastidious cleaner. She would be proud of the sparkle on the chrome. *What would my parents think of Steve's conversion of their retirement home into a chalet bungalow with a proper upstairs and an ensuite master bedroom?* I wonder.

My thoughts return to Lucie. *I will tell her about her father tomorrow, once we've sorted everything out for Maisie.* I pray that Maisie will have done well enough to take A-levels. I'm also fully prepared with a backup plan: the last-minute rounds of college courses and apprenticeships.

I run bleach around the basin of the toilet and inhale the sharp chemical smell. I can't quite remember why I told Lucie the elaborate and muddled sperm donor and IVF stories all those years ago. I press flush. Of course, it was around the time that Tim and Faith, a couple we used to be friendly with in the village, started their course of IVF resulting in twins. When Steve asked about Lucie's father, the lie just tumbled out and he believed me. Then again, maybe it was a story that was easier for everyone to understand. Come to think of it, Steve has never asked or mentioned Lucie's biological father again. I remember how Steve took to baby Lucie immediately, as if he believed on some level that she was his own.

Thursday 25th August

Maryam

I've never known it to be this hot at night in the UK. The bedroom window is wide open and a warm familiar smell seeps into the room. The combination of earthiness from the nearby river and a fumy oily smell, probably from the traffic, takes me right back to our family estate in Gojra. I remember the cotton ginning machines, which to a then six-year-old me were enormous and frightening, as they set about turning raw cotton balls into cloth to be sold all over the world.

I toss and turn. I wonder if our freshly laundered white sheets are from the white fluffy cotton plants of the Punjab.

But it isn't only the heat which is causing me to lose sleep. I wanted to tell my brother what I'd found out from Professor Schonerts. After all, he deserves to know. Nabeel is part of the story of what happened back then.

Last Sunday morning, the household was busy as usual. Everyone on top of everyone else. But I had a plan to get Nabeel on his own. To tell him face-to-face. I'd convinced Nav to take the kids to the park. Nadiya was in bed and Maneer and Mona were cooking. Luckily, my brother was eager to speak to me alone. He had a whole load of business things he needed to run past me. Business talk over, I was on the point of telling him the professor's discovery when Maneer and his sister wandered into the dining room, followed by Nav back from the park, and the carefully orchestrated moment was gone. I couldn't even have a private conversation in my own home! I was angry, and worse still felt a whole wave of tears well up inside me.

In some ways I'm glad I didn't tell Nabeel just then. I would have embarrassed myself by bursting into tears. Growing up, my brothers were always over-emotional and quick tempered. All these years later Nabeel is still prone to outbursts. I wonder if some of his success is fuelled by what happened back then: the drive and motivation directed into his work, using the last of the cotton money, and a small bank loan to invest in property and save our family from financial ruin.

I know I should speak to Maneer. *The decent thing to do is to talk to your husband first,* says a voice in my head. The thing I've been dreading. I love my life just as it is and don't want to rock the boat. But I owe it to my elder brother. My husband will have heard stories like this before, probably from some of his patients, just not from his own wife.

I look at the clock, it's still too early to do anything. I'm condemned to a few more hours of sleeplessness. *Try and get some sleep!* I tell myself.

Once Maneer wakes I will tell him everything.

Tori

I throw off my bed covers. I haven't slept much at all. Through the window, a clear blue sky beckons. I might as well get up.

Out of habit I reach for my dressing gown and decide it is too warm even at this hour to put it on.

Out through the back door and I inhale the new day. Already the sun is warm on my face. I check the thermometer pinned to the wall. Twenty-one degrees and it isn't even six o'clock. I am taken back to my time travelling the world. The heat and smell of the day doesn't feel like home. It feels faraway. I could be in Cairo or Mumbai. It takes me far away from this little corner of England.

I pad across the grass, feeling the soothing texture of the lawn beneath my feet. I sit at the garden table and am joined by "Mr. Pheasant", as the girls call him. He's waiting for Steve to come and feed him. The stunning colours: red, blue and ochres of his plumage would make a great photograph in this early morning light. "You'll have to wait for breakfast until Steve is up." The bird turns and shuffles off through the gap in the hedge—as if he understands.

Alone with my thoughts I run through the day ahead. It will be like that moment in *The Godfather Part III* when the past is set straight. I've always been a fan of Coppola films, and the day of reckoning has arrived—for both of my daughters. Maisie will collect her exam results and, whatever the outcome, plans to go out with her friends to celebrate. Steve is going down to the pub with his mates to see The Water Rats, a band that tours the Broads by boat. It will just be me and Lucie: a rare opportunity with my eldest these days. I will tell Lucie the true story about her biological father.

Maryam

I have barely slept and feel exhausted. I need to get up and tell Maneer right now. But I need to shower first and wake myself up. He will have to go to work and that will be that. I won't have to face him through the long day ahead.

Maneer

As usual I wake early, a little before sunrise, ready for my prayers. My morning prayer routine has much in common with modern wellbeing techniques purported by my GP colleagues: be mindful, be truly in the moment. Between the beginning of the true dawn and the sun rising, the morning prayer is special, the most sacred, and for others the most testing. The call to *subh* prayer has the additional words, *Prayer is better than sleep*.

Today my prayers don't happen. To be honest I am agitated by the change of routine, like a runner unable to take their morning jog. I don't feel right. It was a disruptive night. I'd woken on and off and found Maryam either tossing and turning, or up and about. When morning finally came Maryam was sitting up already wide awake, which was unusual. I wanted to ask her if she was okay but she got out of bed and went to take a shower.

Maryam looked tired. There were puffy bags under her eyes. She's been acting a little strangely since the weekend. I had put it down mostly to Mona's visit: she was always a little jealous of my close and easy relationship with my sister. But now I feel there is something else. A set of mild symptoms, minor things, which when gathered together—rather like making a clinical analysis—point to some disorder. Possible diagnoses speed through my mind. Is it stress at work? The mayhem of Mona and her kids? The added stress of having her only brother now coming and going to Norfolk for business dealings she doesn't altogether feel comfortable about? Is it that our eldest child is about to fly the nest? So many possibilities.

I go downstairs to start my usual breakfast routine. I need to keep some sense of normalcy this morning. Popping a slice of bread in the toaster, I start to make my favourite beverage—masala chai—just as Maryam walks into the kitchen. I still find my wife beautiful. As beautiful as the day I first set eyes on her at the inter-collegiate chess tournament. Back then I was a King's medic, in the audience supporting my team, and Maryam, the only woman playing for University College London, a twenty-minute walk away in Bloomsbury. My mind flashes back to those sweet memories. I am nostalgically spreading my toast with marmalade when Maryam says, "We need to talk." I sense she wants to say something important, but is struggling, and this makes me feel nervous. *Is she okay? Are we okay? Is it Nav?* I wonder if at seventeen he is too young to go away to university and would benefit from a Gap Year.

There is a long moment, and then she says, "If we are going to go to Pakistan over the Christmas holidays, we need to book a flight soon."

"We can start browsing options," I reply, all the while knowing that this isn't what she really wants to talk about. I see this behaviour with my patients. They'll tell me something factual, when what they really want to talk about is their feelings. Often, they will wait until they've gotten up and gone to the door, only then do they turn back and say, "There's something else I need to tell you about."

I linger over breakfast in the hope that Maryam will say more; but the something else never comes and so I leave for work.

I turn up the volume on the car radio. The newscaster reports that people up and down the country are bracing themselves for the heatwave. It is set to be the hottest GCSE results day since records began. "Try spending the summer in the Punjab if you want to know about heat!" I tell the radio presenter.

Housing estates merge into fields stacked full with hay bales; one square piled on top of another like a Jenga tower. I am late for work, but I don't put my foot down on the gas. I pride myself on being a careful driver, even though my new Range Rover can do crazy speeds. More haste less speed is my motto! And anyway, I am never late for work. Today is an exception.

I indicate right into the surgery car park. I turn over the conversation I had with Maryam before leaving the house this morning. What did she really want to tell me? My stomach clinches. I switch off the engine and take a few deep breaths, all the while watching the heat haze rising across the tarmac. I step out of the climatically controlled Range Rover and blasts of hot air smack me straight across the face. The wraparound heat and dust. I recall a childhood summer visiting family in Pakistan.

The East Anglian farming landscape reminds me a lot of the Punjab. The UK has four distinct areas much like Pakistan. London and the south coast are the mega city of Karachi and the Arabian Sea. Whereas Scotland's rugged mountains and wild weather is the North-West Frontier. To the west is Wales, the lesser-known Baluchistan.

Nav

Aunty Mona and the kids finally left late last night. The drawn-out goodbyes would make a stranger think that they were off to Australia, rather than back home to Manchester. Thankfully she's taking Nadiya and Muni back to stay with her until the end of the holidays. I narrowly escaped joining them, pleading that I needed some peace and quiet to do my reading for Cambridge. This is partially true. The bigger truth would have been to say, "I want to see Lucie, because she is so much more interesting than all of you." That wouldn't have gone down too well, though!

I get up and check myself in the mirror. Stubble. I could grow a beard. A hipster beard like Archie and the newspaper photographer. Except when your beard is black, and your skin is brown, you have to keep a beard closely cropped. Otherwise, people might look at you nervously; see the cliché religious man, from spiritual guru to religious fanatic. *Or am I imagining this?* I'm not sure. I take the electric razor to my face and prepare to meet Lucie.

Lucie

I try on a red floral halter-neck dress I bought from the new boho boutique in town. There's a whole pile of discarded clothes on the bed. Is this better than my denim shorts and T-shirt? *Ugh why is picking an outfit so hard!* I look at my reflection in the floor-length mirror: vibrant red hues and a paisley pattern with dashes of turquoise create a bold summer look and hopefully show I'm into textiles art. *This is the one, now leave before you miss the bus!* I grab my bag and race downstairs.

"Good, you're coming with us," sighs Mum, picking up her car keys. "Your old schoolteachers will be so pleased to see you."

How can she do this? She knows I'm going into town on the bus. This is an awful example of Mum saying one thing and meaning something entirely else. I put on my best surprised face followed by a confused frown. "I'm good. I'm getting the bus into town. My friends are back from holiday. We've organised to meet up." Friends is my code word for Nav and the secret DNA project.

"I can drop you off after we've picked up Maisie's results."

Maisie rolls her eyes behind Mum's back.

"We're going straight to college for A-level enrolment after," continues Mum. "All in all, probably just as quick as getting the bus."

Another roll of the eyes from Maisie, who is being scarily silent today.

"Okay," I say. I follow them to the car telling myself that I'm giving Maisie moral support, rather than doing what Mum wants me to do.

We are in and out of Maisie's school with lightning speed. The teachers wanted to have a talk with Maisie about her future, but Mum was having none of it. She told them she had her own plans for her daughter. Maisie didn't say a word. She was worryingly subdued, not her usual chatty self.

Maisie clutches her results slips. She did as expected in her GCSEs, which isn't great news, and so we are heading towards the city in silence. The radio drones on about the heatwave. This prompts Mum to take her eye off the road and turn towards the back seat and say, "Maisie, did you put factor fifty on?"

"Yes," she hisses.

"You do know you can even get sunburnt in the car," continues Mum. "It happened to me once in Italy!"

Nobody ever mentions the fact that everyone in the house, except for me, all share a large bottle of factor fifty sunscreen. Mum, Dad and Maisie plaster it over themselves several times a day as soon as there's the slightest hint of summer. Factor fifty gives their skin even more of a pale ghostly sheen than normal. For that reason alone, I'm glad I don't have to use it. I'd look like I was wearing white face paint! Mum buys a small bottle of factor fifteen sunscreen just for me. No one ever discusses this disparity. If they did, it would open up the whole gaping crevice of me looking so different to them, as if I belong to a different family altogether.

The newsreader moves on from the heatwave to this year's GCSE results. "The first decline in top grades for years." I switch the radio off. This sort of talk isn't going to help Maisie who hasn't made the grades to study for her A-levels.

Maisie stares out of the back window at the clear blue sky. A perfect summer's day—for some.

Mum fills in the silence by telling me about a new module she's writing entitled: A Short History of the Family Photo.

"Family photographs can be considered cultural artefacts because they document the events which shape families' lives.

The recording of family history is an important endeavour. In many cases, photographs are the only biographical material people leave behind after they die."

I want to say, "How can you say all this when I've never seen what my father looks like?" Lack of empathy, or what?

Mum rambles on as if I'm in her seminar group. "The family photo album is an easy way to initiate outsiders to one's family history. This seemingly primal urge to produce and preserve family pictures is a comparatively recent phenomenon."

We're at the inner ring road. I want to jump out of the car and head straight into town to meet Nav, when a notification flashes up on my phone. *You have DNA matches.* My finger hovers over the message.

Lucie Hansen you've got DNA Matches

I open the message.

Hi Lucie,
Good news! We've discovered new DNA Matches for you.

A pink icon fills the screen. I guess this means I have a female match. A little dismayed I realise this obviously means the match isn't my father. I click again. It says I have a half-sister. Twenty-one per cent shared DNA. I don't believe it! Would this be a sister who looks like me?

Mum changes gear and glances across to my phone. I quickly close the DNA message. I can't wait to tell Nav, my miracle worker! Mum pulls up in the college car park and I jump out of the car, saying, "I'm sure there'll be a course that's just right for you, alright, Mais?"

Maisie doesn't answer. I have a moment of panic about leaving Maisie and Mum together. Please don't tell her about Nav and the DNA test. No, Maisie wouldn't throw me under the bus just to get Mum off her back.

"Yes, I'm sure there will be a BTEC or something," says Mum, touching Maisie's arm. "Or you could do retakes? Look! It says, *Get Yourself Sorted* on the banner," she adds trying to jolly Maisie along.

*

I'm sweating after legging it across town. This heatwave feels like being in the Mediterranean! Nav is sitting with a tall glass of Coca-Cola at a table in the pub garden by the river. I wave and walk over. I smile. He gets up and we hug.

I sit down on the wooden bench opposite him. As soon as I'm with Nav, I feel my nerves settle. "Can I get you a drink?" he asks.

"In a minute. First, I have some exciting news. Can I have a sip?"

"Sure," says Nav pushing the glass towards me.

"You won't believe this," I say. "I've just got a DNA match. It worked! You made it all happen."

"Not me. It's the science," says Nav.

I open the message and read him the facts and figures. "The upshot is I have a half-sister."

I am interrupted by a ping of a text from Maisie.

Not now Maisie! I know it sounds a bit mean, but I quite like the idea of having another sister. Maybe she'll be more like me!

"An older sister would be really cool," I say imagining someone who looks like me and works in the Arts or Media. Someone who gets all my interests. Or maybe it is a younger sister and her parents have sent off her DNA?

"You know a half-sister can have the same DNA percentage as other relatives?"

"What do you mean?" I ask.

"A half-sister would have the same degree of relatedness as an aunt. Doesn't it explain that on the site?" says Nav.

I scroll down through the blurb. My heart is pounding with excitement. "You're right. It says it will depend on a range of factors, such as: date of birth. Hang on a minute. There's more here. My half-sister has a name..." My heart thuds and I am certain that Nav can hear every beat. "She's called Maryam Maneer."

Nav freezes.

"Nav, are you okay? What's wrong? Is it something I've said?"

Jenny

Matt and I are sitting in the back of the estate car on what the French call *un jour de grand départ*. This means holidaymakers across France are all travelling on the same day. My parents mistakenly chose today of all days, for the long drive to the ferry port. I can't wait to get home. I can't believe how much I've missed my friends, especially Lucie.

Mum thought an e-break, her term for staying in a remote Breton cottage, was just what our family needed to relax and unwind together. This is highly embarrassing, and I hate to admit it, but Dad is addicted to Facebook! Last year he posted photos of our every move on the beach in Turkey: Mum in a skimpy bikini, my sunburnt face and Matt changing out of his trunks on the beach. This year Mum was having none of that. Dad's punishment was ten days off the grid, apart from a drive into the nearest town to call Mr. Adams for my A-level results. If my parents had been online, they would have known to leave early to avoid the traffic jams.

"It really sucks when your parents choose a holiday house with no WiFi and you can only get a signal if you walk two miles down the road to a minor hill," grunts Matt.

"I heard that!" says Mum. "You don't look so bad on the outdoor life: tanned face and sea-bleached hair."

Matt grins.

"*Et moi*?" I ask.

"Oh, you just look awful," says Matt, digging me in the ribs.

"Ouch!"

"Stop it, you two!" says Dad, his face anxiously squared onto the road ahead.

The main entertainment on this journey takes the form of Mum sitting with an old-fashioned car atlas on her lap and giving directions to St Malo. This causes Dad's usual bloodcurdling and erratic driving to go up a notch.

Finally, we get signal. Everyone in the car jumps. The navigation on Mum's phone kicks into action. The quietly confident voice, which sounds rather like Natalie, my art teacher, instructs Dad to take the next left. We check our phones. A whole load of messages from Lucie arrive. I scroll through, incredulous at my best friend's news.

"Mum," I say. "Can you drop me at Lucie's when we get back to Norfolk?"

"What, before going home and having the night in your own bed? And what about collecting Mr. Dibber from the cattery?"

"I forgot about Mr. Dibber," I lie.

"He's *your* cat!" squeals Mum. I just want to see Lucie far more than collecting my cat.

"Can't you see Lucie tomorrow? What's so urgent?" asks Mum.

I am about to reveal all and tell everyone in the car that Lucie has found out about her biological father, just like on that TV show, *Long Lost Families*, which Mum loves so much, when I stop myself. Dad will plaster it all over Facebook.

"I can drive you over once we've collected Mr. Dibbs," says Matt. "If Dad's had enough of driving." Matt's funny like that, he's only a year older than me, and we often squabble as if we're still little, and then occasionally he acts like my much older brother.

"Thanks," I say, remembering how Matt always had a thing for Maisie.

Tori

I open my laptop and type. It doesn't take long before I pause to gaze out of the study window. The hay bales and bottle green trees are a timeless landscape. I'm living in a John Constable painting. Or actually, more like a Charlie Waite photograph! I could imagine one of his colour photographs of this very view. He's so good at capturing a scene, where you feel as if you could walk right into the landscape. *Try and concentrate!* I tell myself. By this point in the summer holidays, I am usually full of enthusiasm for the autumn term. This year will be different; Lucie will fly the nest and be an art student in London—just like I once was.

I'd always told myself that I would talk to Lucie about her father before she left home. Today, in the car, was yet another missed opportunity to talk about all those photographs I took of him: the man I closed the door on, claiming he was an anonymous sperm donor. I had hoped to perfectly transition from the photography module about family portraits into a chat about Lucie's father, but I ended up sounding like a robot reading an essay out loud. Nerves got the better of me. Maybe, somewhere in my subconscious, he was the reason I jumped at the chance to teach this module. Through work, maybe it felt like I could exorcise this ghost from my past.

But how could I have said anything with Maisie in the car, too? There have been so many almost right times, but usually Steve or Maisie are around, and this conversation needs to be strictly between me and Lucie.

When I think about Lucie's father it feels as if I am recalling a character in a novel or film, rather than someone I knew intimately. I would title it: a summer romance in the city. The blurb would read: it began as a chance encounter, and then he became the photographer's muse.

*

Back in the day, working as a young and carefree photographer searching for interesting subjects, I was in London after travelling in Asia and the Middle East, taking my portfolio around magazine offices looking for commissions. I had sold a photograph to *National Geographic* and my career was on its way. *Time Out* was doing a feature on the diverse faces of London. They were after a *National Geographic* look. The right lighting, a graphic composition and good colour contrast, all the ingredients of the exceptional photographs you see in a *National Geographic* magazine.

I was in luck. The original photographer had pulled out and I had an afternoon to complete the job. I had the brainwave of going to SOAS, the School of Oriental and African Studies, to look for likely subjects. It was on my way back through Russell Square that I saw the man who became Lucie's father. He was sitting on a park bench sketching. His face intrigued me. I approached him and asked if I could take his picture.

After the photo shoot we bonded over meals. Our favourite place was a large Chinese restaurant in Soho where the food was delicious and cheap, and served with complimentary jasmine tea. The only drawback was the legendary rudeness of the staff. The service didn't bother us; it was all part of the entertainment. There were evening walks to Brockwell Park gazing dreamily at the city skyline, when he confided in me his hope to one day go to art school. We often took the bus to Brixton Hill and danced the night away on The Fridge's massive dance floor. How he loved to dance!

There's a banging on the study door. "Mum, I can't find my phone charger!" yells Maisie.

Lucie

I'm fizzing with excitement when Jenny's brother drops her off at our house.

"Got my overnight bag," laughs Jenny wheeling in her enormous holiday suitcase and giving me a hug. "So, tell all!"

"In a minute! When we get upstairs."

"Your mum doesn't know?" whispers Jenny.

I shake my head.

"Know what?" says Mum wafting by.

"Girl stuff!" I say.

"Mrs. Hansen, Mum sent this," says Jenny changing the subject and handing over a pretty circular box. "The Camembert got a bit hot in the car."

"French cheese is all the better for being ripe," says Mum. "You look gorgeous," she adds.

Mum's right. Jenny does look amazing with her light tan and sun-kissed golden-brown hair pulled up in a bun.

Finally, I shut the door and we flop down on my bed. "Tell me everything, right from the beginning! DNA. The guy who helped you. The lot," says Jenny.

I'm not sure where to start. I recount the whole thing about sending off the test to find out about my ethnicity. The waiting for the results, my phone saga and Nav. Result: Irish, Scandinavian, English and tiny bit Scottish and the biggest chunk, half South Asian.

"This is truly amazing!" says Jenny. "I will have to completely rewrite you in my mind. How does it *feel* to know about your father's country of origin?"

"South Asia isn't a country, but it's still a kind of relief. I hated the *not* knowing."

"Aren't these things supposed to make you all confused and mixed up?"

"I feel, it sounds a cliché, at peace. I'm still *me*, but there's also another *me*. The two sides of me were both there all along. I'm finally put back together."

"Oh, Luce." Jenny gives me a hug.

'Can I ask something?'

"Sure."

"So, why did your mum say your father was a sperm donor?"

"Maybe he was. I still don't know *who* he is. That's the next piece in the puzzle. It wasn't ever my intention to track him or any relatives down. All I wanted to know was where I was from. It would be a one in a million chance of ever finding out about my father. But Nav uploaded my data onto this match site, and I've found a relative!"

"What a cousin ten times removed?" jokes Jenny.

"No! A half-sister or aunt."

"Really? How can she be a half-sister *or* aunt? I don't understand."

"According to Nav, a half-sister or aunt will both have the same amount of linked DNA. And importantly I now know their family's country of origin: Pakistan," I explain.

Jenny shakes her head. "This is just so amazing! It's like you're living in a movie!"

"The movie's happening around me!" I steel myself to tell Jenny the bit I couldn't put in a message. "I haven't quite told you everything. I met up with Nav and told him about the half-sister thing. I was so excited. After all, it was Nav who'd helped me to find out more. After I told him I'd found a half-sister he was cool with it and explained it could also be an aunt. Then I told him the name, Maryam Maneer. He went quiet. Very quiet. He said, "My mother is called Maryam Maneer.""

"His mother!" says Jenny. "That means you could have a blood relative living just a few miles away from you. Hang on a minute, though. Isn't your friend Nav, called Nav Chowdery? He isn't Nav Maneer?"

"Well remembered," I say.

"It was in the newspaper article."

I am always impressed by Jenny's unusual ability to memorise things she reads. Consequently, she does brilliantly at exams.

"Unless his parents are unmarried?" suggests Jenny.

"No. I mean yes, they are married. Their surnames work differently from ours."

"What, like in Iceland?" says Jenny. "Girls take their mother's name and boys their father's. I'd be Jenny Angleasdottir and Matt would be Matt Keithsson, which he would hate!"

"And me?" I ask.

"Lucie Torisdottir, of course. As Tori is your mother's name and dottir means daughter in Icelandic so they put it all together for your surname."

"I'd be alright in Iceland then, only knowing about my mum. Anyway, I googled Pakistani surnames. They don't work like ours, *or* those in Iceland. I'll show you," I say, looking it up again.

"It says a Pakistani name consists of a given name, sometimes a middle name, and a surname. Unlike in the West, there are many naming conventions. In Islam all humans are equal and family names were discouraged since it implied inequality and division. Apparently all of this is fine in Pakistan but can cause problems in the West."

"I think I get it," says Jenny frowning. "But why would it cause a problem here?"

"Because you wouldn't know who was related to whom! That's why I didn't make the connection either! Nav's mother took her husband's first name as her surname when they married. But then they decided to anglicise themselves when the children were born. Nav's siblings all have the same surname—their father's—so they can fit in better. Whereas, in the past, or in Pakistan, each child would have a different surname, usually in memory of a family member."

"That's so cool," says Jenny. "Don't you sometimes think we're a bit shut off from the rest of the world living in Norfolk?"

"Yeah, I'm so glad I'm moving to London where I can meet more people from different cultures."

Jenny lounges back on my bed. "I never knew any of that about Indian and Pakistani surnames. I wouldn't want to be called after my Uncle Brian. Jenny Brian. No way! Jenny Hemingway, or maybe J Hemingway, will be a much better name when I'm selling my paintings for a fortune!"

After a few minutes silence, Jenny sits up again and continues.

"But back to your long-lost relatives. Couldn't there be loads of Maryam Maneers?"

"In theory yes, but Nav knew his mother's data was on the site."

"Let me get this straight. There is a like ninety-nine point nine per cent probability that your father is the brother of Nav's mother." Jenny's eyes are popping with incredulity. "How many brothers has she got?"

I sigh. "I don't know. Nav left in a sulk."

"Boys!" exclaims Jenny.

"The thing is Mum could still be telling the truth about my father being a sperm donor. People do it all the time to earn money, it's easier than a bank loan. So maybe the sperm donor thing is true and some uncle of Nav's needed money, and never met Mum. Anything is still possible. How can I bring that up with Mum?"

"I hate to say it, but you and your mum *are* going to have to talk about this," says Jenny. "You've got to speak to her sooner or later."

Jenny sounds so grown up and sensible. Even though I know she's right I shake my head. "I can't. I just can't do it. I've been brought up to never mention it. How do you change a habit of a lifetime?"

"But you've got so far. Isn't this the last piece in the puzzle? Don't you want to know if your parents even met? Or if he was some guy strapped for cash who sold some sperm?"

"Do I really want to know?" I mumble.

"Well, one thing you do know is that Nav's your cousin. You have a mate who you happen to be related to."

"I did have a new friend. But after he cleared off, I messaged him asking if I could meet his mother."

"And?"

"No reply. Radio silence."

"Perhaps he didn't get your message," says Jenny smiling unconvincingly.

"Rubbish! Messages don't get stuck in the air, like a parcel lost in the post. Unless, that is, he's gone somewhere off the radar."

"Like rural France!" sighs Jenny.

"In a way it doesn't matter whether one of his uncles, my father, was a sperm donor and doesn't know I even exist. What I want to know is things about their heritage, now it's narrowed down to this part of Northern Pakistan. What is their culture: food, art, famous people? Now that it's part of my culture too. That would mean so much."

"Are you really sure you want to find out?" asks Jenny.

"Yes, I'm sure," I snap. I had always wanted to know who my biological father is, now I have come this close, I'm scared. What if he doesn't want to know me?

"I don't want you to get hurt. What I mean is everyone's family is weird. On holiday I'd have given anything *not* to be related to Mum and Dad!"

Jenny props herself up on my mountain of colourful cushions and fiddles with the appliquéd panels. "I remember when you bought these from that shop in the city where they import all those gorgeous things from India. Did you just like the colours and patterns, or do you think your subconscious knew you were connected to the Indian subcontinent?"

"No idea!" I say.

"Anyway, how many uncles does Nav have? Do you have a shortlist of possible fathers? It's like that scene in *Mamma Mia* when Sophie narrows it down to three possible fathers!"

"Maisie thinks it's like the *Mamma Mia* story too. I have no idea how many brothers Nav's mum has. After he didn't reply to the first message, I sent him another. I asked: how many uncles do you have? What are their names? He didn't reply."

Part of me wants to tell Jenny that I've met one of his uncles already. That Nav's Uncle Nabeel is on the shortlist of possible fathers. I think of Nav's uncle. The way he looked at me. He was really staring at me, as if he recognised me from somewhere and just couldn't quite think where he'd seen me before. My head wants to tell Jenny about meeting him, but something stops me from saying that my father may be a millionaire property tycoon.

"Enough of me. Tell me about your holiday in France?" I say.

Nav

Sitting around the table with my parents for dinner today is excruciating. I don't know what to do. You never get these moral dilemmas when you're studying maths. That's why I was so relieved to give up English—all those debates and decisions!

Earlier today I walked past Mum and Dad's bedroom. I heard the words DNA loud and clear through the closed door. I stopped. Was she talking to Dad?

"Mathilde, what should I do?" asked Mum.

She was clearly on the phone! Strange, though, Mum never asks anyone for advice.

"A long-lost half-sister or niece isn't something I had expected or planned for," said Mum. That was such a Mum thing to say. She used to make a spreadsheet of what we were going to do on holiday, until Dad said, "Stop planning and just go with the flow for once."

Mum doesn't do going with the flow. Mum lives by planning and attention to detail.

Dad came out of the bathroom, and I jumped. "Are you alright?" he asked.

"I'm good," I lied.

I spend the rest of the day trying to keep out of Mum's way. I need to own up and tell her that I know the person she is related to. That would also mean telling Mum about putting Lucie onto the university DNA site. Maybe I should tell Lucie first?

I wait until Mum is alone and stacking the dish washer. "Mum, can we speak?"

"That sounds ominous. What have you been up to?"

"Nothing," I pause. "I don't know where to start."

"At the beginning," says Mum. "Shall we go out to walk and talk?"

"Sure," I say, at least I won't have to look her in the eye if we're on a walk.

Saturday 27th August

Lucie
My phone pings.

> Nav: Hey

> Lucie: Hey

I look up from the futon in Jenny's room. It's so nice to not be at home, to be staying over at the Hemingway's house, even if it was only yesterday morning that Jenny went home from mine! "Jen, I don't believe it! Finally, a message from Nav."

"And?" asks Jenny.

"I can see that he's typing." Is he writing an essay? The anticipation is getting to me and I'm tempted to call him.

> Nav: Sorry for the silence. I didn't know what to do. As you probably guessed my mum is your aunt. I still can't quite take it in.

> Lucie: Does she want to speak to me?
> Will she tell me about my father?

> Nav: Yes. But the thing is she wants to
> speak to your mum first. Is that okay?

This isn't okay, but what can I do? Be patient, the puzzle is almost solved, I tell myself.

> Lucie: Sure.

> Nav: Could you send your mum's number?

> Lucie: I'm staying over at Jenny's.

> Nav: You can still send the number, can't
> you? Mum wants to contact her right now.

> Lucie: Okay. I'll send it over.

> Nav: Cool. Speak soon!

I have a sinking feeling in my stomach.

"What's happening?" asks Jen.

"Nav's mum is my aunt! She wants to speak to Mum. She wants her number. I said I'd send it. But I'm not sure about this. Should I speak to Mum first? I haven't even told her that I've taken a DNA test! What do I do?"

"You ought to call your mum," says Jenny.

"Part of me is desperate to speak to her about all this, but another part of me just doesn't know where to begin."

Tori

I am sitting in bed reading the latest biography of the photographer Dora Marr, when my phone pings. I pick it up off the bedside table. A message from Lucie.

> Lucie: Linking you up with a friend's mum. She might message you. She's called Maryam.

There's no further explanation beyond the name of the woman: Maryam, or is that a typo and she means Mary? Is she wanting to join my book group, or more likely wanting some advice about taking photographs? Curious.

Maryam

I am at my desk in the study. I am enveloped in the past: old whispers of my brother Hanif and "the gori". Gossip and rumours I've spent years trying to forget, which every so often bubble to the surface. I don't feel brave enough to speak directly to Tori, so I begin with a text message. I reason it would give her a moment to process things before we speak, especially given that Nav had said he wasn't sure how much Tori knew, if anything. I explain that Lucie took a DNA test which brought up a close match with my own. I know writing a text might seem too factual and a little frosty, but part of me also feels that it is inappropriate to discuss my brother in an intimate way with someone I have never met.

Tori

Steve is fast asleep beside me. He is snoring faintly, his chest gently rising and falling, I'm glad my husband is beside me. His physical presence is reassuring, even if he is asleep and oblivious to the messages arriving from Maryam.

I am surprised that I'm not more shocked about being contacted like this, out of the blue. Or by the fact that Lucie has taken a DNA test without telling me. *Where did she get the money from?* is one of the first things which spring to mind. *Aren't these tests really expensive?* I do know that my mother-in-law is always in the habit of giving the girls money when she sees them.

Maybe part of me has been expecting something like this to happen sooner or later? I never knew if Hanif told anyone about our relationship, or the news of my suspected pregnancy. But I've watched enough episodes of *Long Lost Family* to know that, with the advances in DNA testing these days, the past doesn't stay in the past.

Maryam

I share facts with Tori, as if explaining DNA to one of my students. Very casually I tell her that Hanif sadly passed away a long time ago.

Tori

I am winded by this curveball. Hanif is too young to be dead! A pain rises up in my chest and I find it hard to breathe. Even though Hanif left me, I'm not bitter. I'd always hoped that he'd found his way and had a good life, too.

I am wide awake and need to talk; I need a way to process this. There are so many unanswered questions about Hanif. He was Maryam's elder brother, my ex, and Lucie's father. Even using his name feels strange after such a long time. What's more, and I didn't expect this, I feel both high and giddy on this intimacy with his sister, the way others might talk on a dating app and furiously exchange messages. But there's something missing in this flurry of messages. For a brief time, back then I believed I'd found my soul mate, yet now it's been such a long time since I had thought about him as a real person, rather than a ghostly memory, I can't quite connect with the man I once felt so close to. I want to hear Maryam's voice.

> Tori: Can I call you?

> Maryam: Of course.

> Tori: I mean now?

> Maryam: Absolutely!

> Tori: Give me a few minutes.

Quietly and carefully, I roll out of bed. Steve snuffles. I freeze, as still as a statue. *Please don't wake up!* As soon as his breathing and intermittent snoring return to normal I throw on my bright red kimono dressing gown and softly pad down the stairs and into the kitchen.

Maryam picks up after the second ring. My heart is pounding. "Hi. It's me, Tori," I say.

"Maryam."

"Thank you for letting me call. I know it's late."

"How did you first meet my brother?" asks Maryam. The woman's voice is clear and precise and has the faintest of Brummie accents. I wasn't expecting her to be so to the point. I thought we'd talk about the fact that it's almost midnight, or maybe comment on the weather, before moving on to Hanif.

"I'm not sure where to begin." I pause. "It all started when I was freelancing back in the nineties, people said I was one of the up-and-coming photographers. Just before the internet and all things digital took over. I had a heavy SLR camera which I'd take everywhere."

"Yes, I remember cameras were never something you could fit in your back pocket. And we had to wait days to actually see the photographs!" says Maryam.

"I used to print my own. Dark room and all that. I had a commission to look for diverse and interesting faces in London. All ages and races. A real open brief and dream of a job. I went to the School of Oriental and African Studies hoping to find interesting subjects for the magazine article."

"Next door to where I was studying at University College of London," says Maryam.

"Yeah, next to UCL." I have a vague memory that I once met Maryam for the briefest of moments. It was a sunny day nearly twenty years ago as we walked past the campus. Hanif and I had been on a few dates by then. He called out to his sister, who came over to us in a fluster. Somehow, I had forgotten this, erased his sister from my mind. We weren't that much older than Lucie is now. We didn't pay that much attention to each other. Back in those pre-internet days we couldn't follow up the encounter with a friend request. Life was all in the here and now. And then lost, forever. What I remember is how beautiful she was, in quite an unassuming and unknowing way. And then she was gone, off to a lecture or tutorial. If Maryam had been there the day I first saw Hanif, I might well have taken her photograph too!

"The day I first met Hanif I already had some good shots of people chatting in happy huddles, and solitary students sitting on the stone terraces lost in thought. There were students from all over the world. Perfect for the commission. Then walking back through Russell Square I spotted some elderly people doing Tai Chi on the grass—ideal photography subjects. I sat down on a park bench and adjusted my shutter speed and reeled off some action photos. It wasn't until I was putting my lens cap back that I noticed the man sitting on the far end of a bench sketching the trees."

"Hanif," sighs Maryam. "He always loved to doodle."

"He was good at drawing. But it was his face that intrigued me. I couldn't quite place it. There was something that reminded me of the people I'd met in the north of India: the smiling eyes and high cheekbones. I asked him if I could take his picture. He said yes. That's how Hanif and I got talking. He was really interested in photography—or said he was," I add, a little annoyed at the bitter tone entering my voice. I want to stay neutral, calm and controlled.

"He was always the one who took the family photographs. These days you'd say that he had a good eye," says Maryam.

"Anyway, Hanif asked if I'd show him the picture. After handing in the contact strip to the picture editor, I printed off the photographs and found him on the same park bench. We went to the little café in the park. And that was the beginning of our relationship."

The conversation about Hanif flows effortlessly and it feels good to talk about our shared past, one I now see we both tried hard to forget so that we could move on. We talk into the early hours of the morning; we create a safe space to finally share our feelings and love for Hanif, for Lucie's father.

We send photographs to fill in any gaps. Lucie is the spitting image of the younger Maryam. We talk about Lucie. We talk about our other children. We soon know every detail of our off-spring's passions and dreams. We talk about our husbands, and about working as lecturers, and our interests in photography and mathematics. I feel an affinity with Maryam.

Eventually the one thing about Hanif which we haven't discussed has to be raised. "So, what happened to Hanif?" I ask. "You mentioned that he'd passed away?"

"Yes, forgive me, this is always very hard to talk about," says Maryam.

"Do I need to be worried about Lucie? Did Hanif have a genetic illness?"

"I understand your concerns, but I think we need to discuss this in person. Lucie should be there too. After all Hanif was her father," adds Maryam. "No more secrets."

We arrange to meet at Maryam's house on Monday afternoon. Maryam and Nav plus me and Lucie.

I run the cold tap and fill a glass with water. I down it in one before making my way back upstairs to bed. I have no idea how I will get to sleep.

Sunday 28th August

Lucie

Sunlight floods in through Jen's bare window. I can't believe its morning. I want to go back to sleep. This bedroom is my second home, and I know every bit of it as well as my own. The room is an exhibition of Jenny's artwork—most from when she was at high school and still into painting flowers. Light dances across the hand-painted roses and trellis decorating the walls, a pretty amazing country garden mural she painted when she was ten years old. Such a talent! Mrs. Hemingway won't allow it to be painted or wallpapered over. "When Jen's famous it'll be like having a Banksy," she says.

Jenny sits up and rubs her eyes and flicks her mane of hair out of her face. "Mum needs to put the curtains back up soon," she groans. "Always the same when we come back from holiday; Mum goes on a cleaning frenzy. It feels like we're camping when the light wakes you up at the crack of dawn!"

"Jen, I don't really want to go home," I say looking up from the futon. I wish I could prolong my sleepover, or better still move in with the Hemingways until I go to art school.

"You're going to have to speak to your mum sooner or later," says Jenny. "Face the music and all that."

"Why can't I just have a normal family, like you?"

"You think our family is normal!" laughs Jen.

I'm too ashamed to even tell my best friend about how I feel like there's something wrong with me. Something wrong about not having a normal family history. At primary school we had a family tree project, and I could only draw one side of it. I felt so ashamed and different to everyone else in the class. But I don't ever tell anyone this.

"What I want to know is whether Mum and Nav's mother have spoken to each other yet? And more importantly, when are any of them going to speak to me? I hate the way this has all become about Mum, and Nav's mother too. Mum is so selfish, keeping everything from me for so long. Does she never think of me for a moment?"

"Yeah, you're right," says Jen nodding in agreement. "It's like parents think their feelings are more important than ours just because they're older! Why is it such a big deal? They have their lives all sorted. Jobs. Money. Relationships."

"It isn't Mum who has had to live with eighteen years of not knowing. Sperm donor or actual father, every time I look in the mirror, or someone asks, 'Where are you really from?' I'm right back in my class at primary school, looking like an idiot."

"Hey, Luce, I have an idea. Why not ask Nav if he knows what's going on? If they've spoken," suggests Jenny.

"You're right! Why didn't I think of that?"

"I'm not just a pretty face," says Jen.

"That's true! Jen, you're beautiful on the inside and out," I say in a sudden rush of love for my best friend. I text Nav and hope he's awake this early in the morning.

Lucie: Hey, you awake?

Nav: Yeah, just woke up.

Lucie: Any updates yet?

Nav: I'm not sure. When I went to the loo in the middle of the night, there was a light on and voices coming from Mum's study.

I love the way Nav is just so honest and uninhibited.

Lucie: Did you go and listen by the door?

Nav: No way!

Lucie: Had to be our mothers speaking.

Nav: Guess so.

Lucie: What happens next? Am I going to get to meet your mum?

Nav: You should. I like having a new cousin. Let's see what they decide.

Jen is looking at me expectantly. "So…what is Nav saying?"

Before I can speak there's a banging on the door. "Morning girls," calls Mrs. Hemingway. The door creaks open. "If you want a lift home, I can take you in half an hour. I need to go into the office. Save you getting two buses back to Reedby!"

"Is that okay? Yeah, thanks so much," I say. There are buses from Jenny's every ten minutes into the city. That's the advantage of living in the suburbs. It's getting to Reedby that can take all day! I rummage round for my bag and toothbrush.

"Hang on," says Jen. "What did Nav say?"

I read the texts aloud. Jen looks thoughtful. "Do you want me to come back with you?" she says.

"I'd love you to come back with me. But I think I have to do this alone." Then as if Mum is actually listening in to our conversation a message arrives. I look down at my phone. "It's from Mum."

Jenny raises her eyebrows.

> Mum: Are you coming back this morning? Do you need me to collect you? I can make us coffee and croissants for brunch.

> Lucie: All good. Mrs. Hemingway is dropping me back soon.

Why can't Mum just say she wants to talk to me?

We stand on the doorstep. Jen is still in her pyjamas. She gives me a hug goodbye.

"Remember, whatever happens, you are still you."

"Yeah," I gulp.

"You're still my beautiful, clever, artistic best friend, Lucie."

There's a beep and I rush to the car. "Are you okay?" asks Mrs. Hemingway.

"I'm good," I lie settling into the passenger seat. "Just a bit tired," I add, which is true!

"You girls, I don't know what you find to chat about into the small hours," she laughs. If only Mrs. Hemingway knew!

Tori

I am slumped over the kitchen table. I'm exhausted both physically and emotionally. Maryam's parting words: "No more secrets," hang heavy over me. Maybe there is a good reason for secrets and closing the door on the past. Yet since our long phone call in the night, all I can think of is Hanif.

Our relationship was no love at first sight like in the movies. It was more like intrigue at first sight. Hanif wanted to see the photographs, so we went to the café in the park. It was run by an Italian family, and they served the best coffee for miles around. The aroma of freshly brewed coffee filled the café. I ordered cappuccinos which we took outside and found a free table. It was better to see the images in daylight. I proudly laid out the black and white contact strips on the wrought iron table and passed him the magnifying glass.

He studied the images. There was a frown on his face where I'd expected to see an impressed smile. After all, I'd been to art school and was a professional photographer. "What do you think?"

"The composition is best on this one," he said looking unimpressed with the photographs I'd taken of him. "The angle of my profile is reflected in the slats on the bench. I like the way they go off the edge of the image."

This wasn't the most flattering shot of Hanif. I was surprised that he could put his own vanity aside and recognise a good picture. Not many people are able to do that. I knew it was the best photograph of him, but it took me several weeks to concede this fact to his face.

I was used to people being slightly disappointed when first seeing a portrait photograph of themselves. "We never see ourselves as others do," was my usual reply.

Photography used to be all about capturing the person in the moment. I hoped to be the next Annie Leibovitz. The American photographer's amazing images of workers on top of the Empire State Building were as engaging as her quirky photographs of actors and musicians. I wrote my thesis on Leibovitz's magazine photograph featuring a nude John Lennon curled up alongside a fully clothed Yoko Ono. It was the last photo ever taken of Lennon, as he was shot a few days later. Annie's photographs always brought out that special something in a person. If Leibovitz were alive today, all her subjects would want to be touched up, any blemish removed and made perfect, whatever that means. The perfection of capturing the moment has been truly lost. Is Annie Leibovitz turning in her grave at the social media saturated world in which we now live? I don't understand why teenagers, including my own daughter Maisie, would use filters to try and look just like everyone else.

"But…," said Hanif, a smile washing across his face. "This picture has it! What's that French word for that indescribable quality?"

"*Je ne sais quoi,*" I said.

"That's it. It isn't really about the tonal range, or even the composition. You just want to keep looking," he said gazing at the image of people practising Tai Chi in the park.

Hanif could have been an artist, or even a gallery curator. But that's all gone now, I think filling the kettle. It's all gone, so how on earth do I begin the conversation with Lucie about her father? I don't even know how he died; simply that it was a long time ago. What I do know is that he just vanished from my life.

I turn a tea bag round and round in the boiling water. My mind is stuck in overdrive. What if he died from some incurable genetic disease? What will any of this knowledge do to Lucie? A whole day and night to wait before meeting Maryam feels interminable. The phone call and planned meet up aren't enough. I need answers before Lucie gets back from her sleepover. I head into the privacy of the garden and call Maryam.

"Sorry to disturb you," I begin nervously.

"Are you and Lucie still good for tomorrow?" asks Maryam.

"Yes," I say, even though Lucie isn't back from Jenny's yet and I haven't had a chance to speak to her.

"I'm sorry I can't talk right now," says Maryam. "I'm in the lab."

"Oh, okay, sorry. We can talk later," I say, wondering what on earth she is doing in her lab on a Sunday morning. I end the call a little annoyed at myself for needing to apologise. This isn't like me. I'm confident and used to talking to friends and colleagues about all kinds of topics. But my past makes me feel nervous and not quite like myself. Perhaps I'm just nervous about speaking to Lucie. I've protected my daughter, shrouding her past in a veil of deceits. I always believed that mine and Steve's love for Lucie was enough to cover over the past.

Steve throws a holdall into the van. "Got to go!" he calls across the drive.

"It's Sunday!" I shout. *What is this with everyone working through the weekend?*

"Sorry. I'm behind on the shower job. I did tell you. Probably back late tonight."

"I'll save you some dinner," I say. The van crunches over the gravel. I am relieved that he is going to be out all day. I need to speak to Steve, but I can't do that until I know the whole story; until I have met Hanif's sister face-to-face with Lucie by my side. Steve has never been interested in the past. He lives firmly in the present. I want to be able to make my own impressions and view about it before sharing with my husband. For me, it feels a bit like when you see a photograph for the first time, if you listen to someone else's opinion, or read the curator's blurb, it somehow influences your own response.

I catch sight of myself in the kitchen window. I'm in my dressing gown and flip flops and my hair is lank and greasy. *I need to get a grip!* I head upstairs for a shower. *Clean hair and a dusting of bronze eye shadow and mascara will do the trick.*

Maryam

The lie to Tori about being in the lab this morning makes me feel uncomfortable. I don't usually tell lies. I am at home.

After all, it is a Sunday! And as a mathematician, even when I am on campus, I seldom venture into a lab, but luckily Tori fell for it.

I could have met both mother and daughter today. It is the holidays, and although I'm busy working on a new paper on the mechanics of motion, I could have made time to see them. In my opinion, telling lies is a waste of time. I used to tell my children that they would always be found out in the end. I remember a saying I grew up hearing, "*jhoot key paun nahin hotey*," that lies don't have feet, so it's not long before the deceptions falls flat on its face. But I was stalling for time: I need a day and a good night's sleep to compose myself before meeting Lucie.

I see myself as a straightforward and logical person. I've worn my hair tied back in a practical ponytail since I was nine or ten years old. I dress in jeans and a shirt at home and for work, unlike some of my colleagues who are much more comfortable in a business suit. Today I feel all over the place and uncomfortable in my body.

Out of routine I switch on my computer and check my work emails. Maneer doesn't like it when I work during the holidays and at the weekend. He says I should take a proper break, but I don't like these long August days. Holidays and a lack of structure always make me uncomfortable. The email trails aren't helping. I can't focus. My past is being rewritten and I'm discombobulated as if I've been spun around in a centrifuge and come out as something quite unexpected and different. In science and mathematics there are prizes for finding formulas and answers to things we believe to be true, things which are in our periphery vision. Now I'm finding answers to Hanif's life before he died and there is a similar sense of discovery and wonder.

My mind searches for the comfort of other mathematical explanations to figure out why I am feeling so out of sorts. It's a similar sensation to being out of space and time when you step off a long-haul flight. The best word to describe this weird feeling is jet lag. Einstein had a lot to say about time: past, present, future. I feel like an astronaut going very fast through space and the seconds ticking by more slowly for an earthbound observer; actually, maybe time dilation is the perfect term for this moment.

I could ring Tori back and tell her this, but I know that Lucie's mother wouldn't appreciate this way of talking: most people don't, and this has made friendships spare and difficult over the years. Nav would understand. I think warmly of my son who seems to have inherited the best of me. I will tell Nav to be home tomorrow afternoon. I still have no idea how to tell my husband any of this.

It was all so long ago, and yet feels like yesterday. Nav and Lucie are almost as old as we were back in the day; me an earnest student visited by her brother and that fleeting meeting with Tori, the girl with long auburn hair dressed in tie-dyed hippy style clothes, even though it was the nineties and not the 1960s!

Maneer

I sit at the sunny garden table and savour my masala chai, enjoying my day off. This is the life: a large period home in a sought-after part of the city, a fulfilling job, and three happy and healthy kids. But there's always something which is a blemish in my near-paradise. I accept this as the way of the world. I like my receptionist, Marg's Buddhist explanation to all this: "The circular yin-yang symbol represents the interconnectedness of the world; there can be no positivity without a negative and vice versa. The seed of unhappiness is in our happiness, and happiness in our unhappiness."

This time, that little seed of unhappiness, lies with my wife. I know Maryam hasn't been herself for a while; she's been especially off-kilter since that Saturday morning when she said she was going in to work. Then last night, when I woke in the early hours, I turned over and found that Maryam's side of the bed was empty. This in itself isn't unusual, as she sometimes gets up in the night and goes to get a drink, and very occasionally she will do an all-nighter working on some university project.

But I was worried and crept downstairs. From her study I could hear Maryam's voice, whispering to someone on the telephone. A tell-tale sign of your wife having an affair, I thought. And yet, Maryam isn't the type to have an affair. But is there ever a type? Part of me wants to pretend nothing is happening with her. Another part of me knows that even though Maryam, usually in jeans and little make up, doesn't think much about her appearance, other people do. She is one of those naturally beautiful women and part of her beauty to me, is that she is always oblivious when people stop and gaze at her admiringly.

Then there is also her magnificent mind, the keeper of so many intellectual accomplishments and insightful thoughts. She is remarkable. That anyone else could be attracted to her is hardly surprising, but is she really capable of an affair? The conversation on the phone sounded in turns intense and intimate.

I reel myself in. This can't go on. We have to talk. I go indoors and stand nervously outside my wife's study door. Then it comes to me. I have recently been on menopause training. Is that, perhaps, it? What sort of GP am I, if I can't even recognise the symptoms of insomnia and mood swings in my own wife? Or is that wishful thinking, something treatable and with the promise of our relationship returning to normal? Of course, it doesn't account for the late-night phone call, nor explain who she was talking to.

I knock and walk in. She looks up. Her brown eyes are a little bloodshot. She looks tired.

"Maryam, are you okay?"

"Of course," she says.

"I mean are you *really* okay? I think we need to talk," I say.

There's a long moment. I am used to waiting for disclosures, so I will myself to not fill the void with idle words.

"I'm sorry," she says. "I should have told you about this a long time ago."

I feel the study walls closing in around me and unsteady on my feet. The words, "a long time ago", aren't what I'm expecting. I pull up a chair beside my wife and take her hand in mine. I let her talk. This is what I am best at doing.

Maryam begins with her brother Hanif and the rumours of him being with an English girl. She tells me about the DNA project and the findings of this research, through to Maryam's conversation with Tori.

A wave of utter exhaustion, followed by relief, washes over me as I kick myself for thinking my wife could possibly be having an affair. I take my wife in my arms and hug her tightly. For all that I'm usually an easy-going doctor with words of wisdom and comfort for everybody's maladies, I don't know what to say to my wife. What I do know is that I have to realign my view of Maryam and her family.

Lucie

There are croissants on the counter…a proper weekend treat!

"Got these out of the freezer," says Mum coming into the kitchen. "Just pop them in the oven for fifteen minutes. Did you have a nice time at Jenny's?"

"Yeah, great!" Mum is wearing make up at home? What's going on? It isn't doing a good job of covering up the dark rings under her eyes. Has she slept at all? I do as Mum says, wondering how we can be talking about defrosting pastries when she looks like she's been up all night. Probably worrying about what she needs to tell me. I wonder if she has spoken to my biological aunt and how that might have gone. I feel really nervous.

Mum places some apricot jam on the table. "Coffee?" she asks.

"Sure," I say. I want to add, "You look like you could do with some caffeine." I am hungry but my stomach lurches and I'm not sure that I want to eat or drink anything at all. I want to get this conversation over with, but I'm waiting for Mum to take the lead. "Are Dad and Maisie around?" I ask.

"Dad's working and your sister's asleep. So it's a good time for us to talk." Mum places a pot of coffee and mugs on the table and sits down. She looks as nervous as I feel. "Lucie, I know about the DNA test. I'm so sorry for not telling you about your biological father. I wanted to protect you. I was going to tell you the truth before you left for art school, but there's never been a good time. I didn't want to muck up your A-levels…"

"That's just an excuse! Mum, I'm not a child anymore!" I snap.

"I know. I'm so sorry," says Mum.

"What is the problem with telling me? Are you embarrassed by me?"

"Never," says Mum looking hurt at the accusation. She takes a deep breath. "Your father was called Hanif. His family came from Pakistan, and they settled in the Midlands. Like you, he loved to paint and draw. We were young and very much in love. I really thought he was 'the one'. But when he disappeared without a trace, I had no choice but to put all memories of him firmly in the past. And gradually he faded from my mind," says Mum, her voice shaking. "We weren't together long. Just a summer romance. I can only remember him now in glimpses of you. You have the same smiling eyes, and focused expression when you are drawing. And of course, your shared love of art." Mum stands and comes over to give me a hug.

"It's okay, Mum," I say, not really sure if I believe my own words. I just want everything to be okay. "It's just, it always felt like there was this whole side to me that we had to pretend didn't exist. People treat me differently to Maisie and I just have to ignore it. I hated hiding this from you, but it's been so exciting to finally acknowledge this other part of myself. I couldn't believe it when I found a match—maybe now I have a chance to feel connected to a family history, especially to all their art and culture; the colours and patterns I've always loved. I want to meet the rest of my family. To meet my father."

"Lucie, there is something else you should know," says Mum unsuccessfully fighting back tears.

"What?" I ask, nervously.

"Your father passed away a long time ago. I'm so sorry you'll never get to meet him. I didn't know either, until a few days ago. I'm so sorry Luce," she says, stroking my hair away from my teary eyes, just like she used to do when I was little and had hurt myself.

A cold wave of shock passes through my body. How can he be dead? This feels so unfair, and cruel too. I came so close to understanding this whole other part of me, and now I feel like I'm back at where I started. This time the unknowing just seems so much worse.

"But he has a sister called Maryam," says Mum. "We can visit her if you'd like. In fact, she's free tomorrow if you'd like to see her." I nod my head as we hold onto each other like we are the last two people left on earth, our quiet sobbing the only sound.

After the conversation with Mum, I don't really know what to do with myself. I don't want to be at home. I don't want to go out. In the end I find myself wandering down to the riverside and Reedby broad. There are tourists sunbathing on the decks of motor cruisers. It's so hot there are even a couple of people swimming in the river.

I sit on a bench and check my messages.

> Jenny: Any news?

> Lucie: So this is what I found out.

I type an edited version of my conversation with Mum, not mentioning that my dad is no longer alive. I'm not ready to say it out loud or type it in a message yet. I only just found out about him, and he's already gone.

> Jenny: Wow! That's amazing. Such good news that your father wasn't just a sperm donor after all. He was into art. Just like you!

Monday 29th August

Nav

I wake early. I sit bolt upright in bed. My shoulders are stiff and tense, and I feel on high alert. For a moment I think it is an exam day, before remembering it's the holidays. I also remember why I am feeling so wound up. Last night Mum knocked on my door and told me about the meeting with Lucie and her mum this afternoon.

"What about Dad?" I said. "Is he going to be there?"

"No, he'll be at work. I've told him about Hanif and his girlfriend. But not much about Lucie. I need to see her first and respect the fact she may want privacy. This is a delicate matter," said Mum, sounding all official.

I told Mum I'm cool with it all, but that isn't exactly true. I said it to make her feel better because she looked so tired and worried. I can't help but think about how this is going to change our family forever. I wonder what Dad thinks about it all? Finding out he has another niece. Maybe he's heard similar stories like this from his patients and really is accepting about it all?

Lucie

I hardly slept last night, I've had so many thoughts; so many stories of my own invention about how today would go. The stories I'd invented as a child: the lost daughter of a Persian prince, the love child of a Spanish artist, the sole heiress to a castle in Italy, are over. The finale is being played out in front of my eyes by real people.

"Maryam will tell you more when we meet her," says Mum, fastening her seatbelt. The radio is playing filling the anxious silence in the car, which is good, as Mum hasn't said as much as I would like about my father, other than the fact that he was an artist and it was a summer romance, and he has since passed away. She said that there was a lot she didn't know either and needs answers herself, but the one thing she has said repeatedly is that I was born out of love, which is nice but also a bit gross—no one wants to picture their parents like that! Nav hasn't said much either, other than that he never got to meet his uncle.

We turn off for the city and into a road of smart Georgian houses. "This one here, on the right," I say.

Mum stands behind me and I knock on the front door. "It's a beautiful house," says Mum nervously.

"Yeah," I say.

The door creaks open and I feel my stomach slipping away from me.

"Lucie," says the woman. She is surprisingly similar to an image that Maisie created of me on her special app which manipulates a photograph to change your age. Now I am seeing myself in twenty years' time in real life!

"Maryam. Aunty Maryam," I say nervously.

She smiles.

"Tori," says Mum. They shake hands and we go inside.

*

Maryam carries a tea tray into the dining room. The French windows are open and letting in a welcome breeze. "How do you take your tea?" asks Maryam, her hand shaking as she pours Earl Grey tea into large floral mugs.

"A dash of milk, no sugar, please," says Mum, looking very pale.

"Same for me," I say, sitting next to Mum on the leather sofa.

Nav gets up and pours himself a glass of water.

Mum and Maryam exchange pleasantries about the weather and when the heatwave will break. Maryam bites her lip nervously. I guess this feels much harder face-to-face than when she was texting or chatting on the phone to Mum. It's weird but I don't feel like a stranger here at all. Not just because I've been here before with Nav, but also because I look so like Maryam. The kink in her hair falling free of her ponytail looks just the same as when I tie my hair back. Our eyes and eyebrows are almost an exact match. This is uncanny.

Maryam takes a deep breath. "As you now know I am Hanif's sister. Lucie, that means I am your aunt."

Mum's mug quivers in her hand. Her face is flushed. She looks like she wants to run out of the room.

"Is everyone okay? Shall I continue?" asks Maryam. She turns to me. "We can stop if you need to take a break or if this gets too overwhelming for you."

"I'm okay," I say.

Mum gazes at Maryam and back at me. "You have the same dark eyes; Hanif's eyes," says Mum.

Maryam takes a deep breath. "There were always rumours that Hanif was seeing an English girl. Back then, for our family this was considered scandalous."

Mum's eyes meet mine.

"Hanif was the eldest, then me, and finally Nabeel, the baby of the family and the smart one. If Hanif had a talent, it was his easy manner, always the family member everyone wanted to be with. He loved to dance at parties. He was also the thoughtful one. Especially where his little sister was concerned," she smiles wistfully.

"Once I began my studies, whenever Hanif was down in London on business, he would drop by my halls of residence in Bloomsbury bearing little gifts: spa products, perfume, chocolates, a scarf. Sometimes he talked about you, Tori. About how much he loved walking around Norwich with you. He wanted us to be friends, to show me the place where he thought he could make a life. He was a good brother, and I have no doubt that he would have been an amazing father."

I smile and for a moment wonder what that would have been like. *Would we have gone out sketching? Would we have gone to exhibitions together?*

"The eighties and nineties had seen a decline in our family's wealth, and with that their status. A good marriage alliance for the eldest son could secure the family's future in many ways." Maryam pauses and looks to Mum. "May I ask when you last saw my brother?"

Mum has a faraway look. "I remember it well. It was a dreary February morning, one of those winter days when it never gets light, when Hanif left my south London flat for the airport," she says.

So it wasn't just *a summer romance*, I think.

"I never saw or heard from him again. What was I to think? He'd deserted me. The ultimate love rat," says Mum, trying hard not to look at me. "I decided I had to put it all behind me and to move on with my life."

"A mixed-race relationship wasn't that easy back then, even with all the celebration of multi-cultural Britain," explains Maryam. "It may not have been the overt racism of the sixties and seventies anymore, but it was still beyond many people's comfort and imagination. He'd have been the first one of a large family marrying out. The family would have likely cut him off. Though, I suppose, we can never know for sure." She swallows hard, takes a tissue from her rolled up shirt sleeve and dabs her kohl lined eyes.

"He just left...it seemed like he'd disappeared into thin air," says Mum, rising to her feet. "Sorry I don't know if I can take much more of this!"

"Mum," I say, "We've come this far. We need to hear the rest."

"Please! I understand how hard this must be for you and Lucie," says Maryam.

Obediently, Mum sits back down.

"As you know he went to Pakistan. But what you don't know is that he came back to the UK a week later. He told our parents he couldn't marry the girl the families had arranged for him. He told them he was in love with someone else."

"What?" Mum looks like the ground beneath her feet has been shaken. "You're not just saying this to make him sound better. Honourable," she says.

This must be so weird for Mum, this sudden rewriting of her past. All I have thought about is the rewriting of my past, not hers.

Nav looks away, shocked by the revelations.

"I'm telling you the truth. And yes, he was honourable," says Maryam.

"But Hanif married her anyway?" says Mum with a shrug, unwilling to completely let go of her belief that he had betrayed her. "And then died a few years ago? Isn't that what happened? He was loyal to his family, but not to me."

"No. It was you. It was *you* more than anyone else he wanted to be loyal to."

"How?" sighs Mum, her eyes welling with fresh tears of loss, hurt and frustration.

"He told our parents he couldn't go ahead with the arranged marriage and they understood, to a point. They didn't disown him. They even pleaded with the girl's family, to the aunt and uncle who'd brokered the engagement, to let the arrangement go. It was then that the pressure cranked up. Her parents realised something was wrong and moved the wedding date forward and to the UK. The young bride was flown from Lahore to Birmingham and she only spoke a few words of English."

Mum stares ahead into space. Nav gazes out of the window. I look down at my sandals. I want to say something, but now this seems more about Mum and Maryam than me. I can finally understand why this has all been so difficult for Mum.

"I took the train home a few days before the wedding ceremony. We had dinner. It was getting dark outside, and Hanif asked me to go for a walk. I think he wanted to talk," says Maryam, swallowing hard. "If only I'd gone with him."

"What do you mean, if only you had gone?" whispers Mum.

"I didn't want to tell you this on the phone, or in a text. And Lucie needs to hear it from me too."

"What happened?" mutters Mum.

"When he didn't come back from that walk, an hour or so later, our father and Nabeel went to look for him. Back then there were gangs of youths who would hang around the towpaths and taunt passers-by, especially if your skin was brown. Nabeel and our father didn't see a soul. They came back empty handed. We suspected he'd fled to be with the *gori*...to you."

"You know that didn't happen!" says Mum. "I didn't expect to be accused of anything. I thought we were here today for Lucie, so she can find out about her heritage."

"This *is* for Lucie! It isn't all about you, Tori," says Maryam sternly. She takes a sip of lukewarm tea and puts the mug down again. "Hanif's disappearance had a domino effect on the whole family. For several weeks his name wasn't mentioned. They assumed he'd run away and overnight Nabeel replaced him as the eldest son. He was eighteen and in his final year of sixth form. He was smart and planned to go to university. He was working weekends and evening shifts at McDonald's to help out. Clever and hardworking. The perfect substitute husband for the young bride."

"She had no say in suddenly having to marry a different man?" I gasp.

"That was the way. Nabeel had no say in it either. He stepped in and saved the family. He married the young bride, Leila. She has a good life. A very good life. She's bright too. If only she'd learn to speak a little more English people would know how smart she is. Sometimes I think it's her brains, not my brother's, behind their success!"

"Success?" asks Mum.

"They made a fortune. With the dowry from Leila's family coupled with a small bank loan Nabeel bought some property. Right time, right place. Birmingham was about to get a facelift and people always need somewhere to live, especially with the growing student population."

A glimmer of a smile passes across Mum's face. "Behind every great man…"

There's a long pause. "And Hanif?" asks Mum.

"The family assumed he'd run off to you." Maryam pauses. "There's no easy way to tell you what happened next."

A shiver goes down my spine. Mum puts her hand on my shoulder. A sense of foreboding. It feels distinctly personal and uncomfortable.

"My brother's body was found floating in the canal five days later by workers on their way to a nearby factory. Hanif had his little sketch book zipped up in his coat pocket. He always carefully wrapped it in a polythene bag in case it rained—he was so protective of his sketchbooks. The inside cover was inscribed with our phone number and address. So the police were in touch straight away."

My heart pounds almost drowning out Maryam's steady voice. *You knew he was dead before you came here today. Don't let the details get to you.* I squeeze Mum's hand.

"The pathologist found nothing suspicious about his body. They told us he simply lost his footing. Before gentrification, the footpaths were uncared for. What caused that to happen, a kerfuffle or just slipping on the muddy bank, we'll never know for sure. Hanif couldn't swim. None of us could—back then. But the reason Hanif was in the water in the first place was left unexplained. The coroner had no choice but to deliver an open verdict."

The atmosphere is as serious and tense as if Maryam is in court on the witness stand like you see in television dramas. "As a close-knit family we were perplexed by the whole saga. We couldn't believe that he was lying dead in a canal for almost a week—not ten-minutes away from our home." Tears slip down Maryam's face for she is unable to keep her composure any longer. For a long moment we are all quiet, too lost in our own thoughts to speak.

"Six months later Maneer proposed to me: a man from a family whose status didn't match ours," continues Maryam. "But nevertheless, he was a doctor and so my parents agreed.

There was no discussion. They weren't going to allow tradition to cause them to lose another child. I never stopped thinking about Hanif, and when an opportunity opened up at the university here, I took it. I wanted to feel closer to my brother and the parts of his life he had loved."

I sit back and collect my thoughts. This is the moment to ask questions, but I am unable to function verbally. My thoughts and feelings are whirling around my head and heart. From moment to moment my past is being continually rewritten. "Are there any photographs of my father?" I finally ask.

Maryam shakes her head. "One day I noticed that we didn't have any pictures of him anymore. He'd been erased from the family story. Tori, do you have a negative of any of the photographs you took of Hanif?"

"Sorry. No, I don't have any prints of him either," says Mum. "I hate to say this, but I had a little bonfire, I lit and burned anything connected to Hanif when he disappeared all those years ago."

Knowing all this feels uncomfortable. I suddenly have a thought. "Mum, the magazine you worked for, they must have an archive?" I ask.

"Unlikely. You see in the end *Time Out* didn't choose the photo with Hanif or the students. They printed a picture I took of people practising Tai Chi early morning in Russell Square. They loved it. It was a very popular image."

For a long minute all is quiet. It is Mum who breaks the silence. "You know Hanif occasionally mentioned an arranged marriage. I was young and the thought of anyone our age marrying seemed crazy. He told me he didn't want to marry the girl that had been chosen for him. Like I said, the last time I saw him was the moment he left for the airport to go to Pakistan. I never saw him again. By the time Lucie was born, I had to put Hanif behind me. I assumed he'd married the girl and never returned to the UK."

There is a long pause, until Maryam says, "My parents tried to support Hanif, but they also felt compelled to keep their word to Leila's family. A girl who's had her engagement cut off can find herself blacklisted for marriage. No matter the reason, people would suspect she was somehow at fault. Her parents were sorry for how things unravelled but everyone was trying to do the right thing by their own families. You and Lucie need to know that."

Mum nods and sits quietly. She opens her handbag and takes out her car keys.

I don't want to go yet. I want to stay longer and absorb all this.

"Wait! Before you go," says Maryam. "Lucie, Nav tells me you are going to study textiles."

"Yeah! I've always loved textiles."

Maryam drags an upright dining chair to the wall and climbs up. She unhooks the wall hanging and steps down, placing the cinnamon-coloured hanging on the table. "I want Lucie to have this. The shawl is an antique. Textiles are in our blood."

"It's beautiful," I say, examining the golden yellow and red stitch work which glows in the sunlight through the window.

"This is a Phulkari. It is a term for embroidery from the Punjab region. It means 'flower work', and at one time was used as the word for embroidery. Over time, Phulkari has come to mean textiles that have been made using this labour-intensive style."

"Do you ever wear it?" I ask.

"Traditionally they are usually worn by women as large shawls on special occasions; Phulkaris were also made as blankets and furniture covers. My grandmother always told me what she loved most was the fact that women of many religious groups: Muslims, Hindus, Christians and Sikhs all stitched Phulkaris together. Young girls learnt needlework from older female relatives and friends. You could call it an emblem of pre-partition life."

My eyes fill with tears. I can't stop them coming.

"But as a young artist, you'll be interested to know that it has also been used in high fashion. There's a designer called Manish Malhotra, who created a Phulkhari based couture collection," adds Maryam placing a hand on my shoulder.

"How did you know that?" asks a surprised Nav. "You're not normally into fashion."

"Nadiya spotted them on Instagram and showed me," says Maryam. "Your sister follows all these fashion designers."

I lay my fingers on the shawl—and my connection with the past. "Do your brother and sister, and the rest of the family know about me?"

Nav shakes his head. "Not yet. Dad does a bit…"

"My husband knows that you exist. That's all I've told him. Are you happy for us to tell them all about you?" asks Maryam.

"Of course," I say, uplifted at the thought of being welcomed into my father's family.

"Let me find something to put the shawl in," says Maryam.

I turn to Mum and Nav. "It's gorgeous! I love it!"

Maryam returns with a large canvas bag. She carefully rolls up the fabric. Light shines in through the window and catches the threads. They sparkle, jewel-like in the eerie twilight of the darkening sky.

"Thank you!"

"You're welcome," says Maryam. "We'll get something new for the wall. It's good to ring in the changes."

"It really is time we made a move," says Mum looking at the stormy sky.

Giant raindrops splash onto the drive and give off that fresh earthy smell. Mum and I make a mad dash to the car.

"I love this smell! The smell of rain on a hot summer's day," I say winding down the car window. Nav and his mum shelter in the porch and wave goodbye.

Mum revs the engine and reverses over the gravel whilst a Range Rover waits to turn into the drive.

Nav

"Was that *them* pulling out of the drive?" asks Dad running into the house to avoid the rain.

"Yes," I say, nervously. "You've just missed Lucie and her mum." I follow Dad into the dining room.

"You're back early," says Mum clearing away the tea tray.

"They say there's going to be flash floods later because the heatwave has left the ground bone dry, so I left after the last patient. I'll finish up my paperwork here." Dad looks around. He's always brilliant at reading a room. If he wasn't a doctor, he'd make a brilliant detective. What is he going to say about the visit from Mum's long-lost family? He gazes at the faded paintwork where the shawl used to hang. "Something's changed."

"A lot has changed," I say, hoping Mum will get the hint and just tell him everything about Lucie sooner rather than later. There's no need to keep being secretive about all this. "Mum gave Lucie Grandma's shawl."

"Good," says Dad. "I'd like to meet them both."

Mum bites her bottom lip.

"Mum's going to tell you more about my new cousin," I say escaping to my bedroom.

Lucie

By the time we hit the bypass, to take the road out of the city, the rain is chucking it down. I'm grateful for the noise of the wipers on double speed and the rain hitting the roof. Mum and I don't say anything. We sit in a comfortable silence as I replay the events of this afternoon in my mind. No doubt, she's doing the same thing too.

We reach the turning for the village and the road has metamorphosed into a fast-flowing stream. "The road's flooded! The water might be deep enough to get into the exhaust," says Mum, turning the car around back the way we came. "Looks like we'll be going home the long way."

Mum pulls out into the road and rather than continuing on the back road home she parks on the verge. "Lucie, I'm sorry," says Mum, staring ahead as if she's still driving.

"Sorry? Sorry for what?" I ask.

"Sorry that I put off telling you about your father for so long. So many things happened back then. Things were different and I had filled all the blank spaces with made up assumptions about his family. I feel awful that I didn't try to find out what had happened. I was so convinced of my own tragedy that it was easier to blame others and make a fresh start with my life. It's you, my love, I let down most. I'm so sorry. We've got a while. So let me tell you some more. Your father was a warm and loving man and knew how to make people feel special. He was kind, which is such an important yet underrated quality. He was quiet but magnetic and so often noticed things that others were just too busy to see. We used to go dancing…"

Eighteen years of nothing and now all this. But I'm not complaining. I'm relieved that everything is out in the open.

My body isn't so cool about all this though. I am shaking and streaming with tears. Both of us are crying. Not sad tears though. More tears of release. As we pull into the driveway, the rain eases and I ask, "What about Dad?"

"I'm so glad you're still calling Steve, Dad," Mum sniffles.

"Of course, he's still my dad! But what are we going to tell him?"

"Leave that to me. I will talk to him," says Mum.

The final piece of the puzzle is in place. No more secrets. My origins are no longer a no-go area. I feel validated. No longer a pretender. No longer an outsider. But I still can't quite believe this isn't a story about someone else. That this is really the story of my life.

Epilogue

2016-2017

First Year at University

Lucie

In the end it is Dad who drives me down to London in his van. There isn't room for Mum or Maisie. Just me and him, and a van full of my stuff: art materials, clothes, rugs, cushions, all the things which will make me feel at home in the halls of residence.

The radio is on for company and Dad has his eyes on the road. We drive by endless flat fields, then as we get closer to the city the landscape fades into a series of nineteen-thirties semi-detached houses and little parades of shops. The London skyline of glass and steel is in view. My heart is racing with excitement. Google Maps gives us just over thirty minutes until our arrival.

"I need to say something before we hit the M25," says Dad. Is this going to be the how to manage your money talk, or the contraception talk? I feel nervous. Jenny messaged me yesterday saying her mum started on about all these things in the car to university.

Dad overtakes a mint-green Fiat 500 and then moves back into the slow lane. "I know I'm not one for sending texts or saying stuff. I'm a do-er."

I nod.

"You know Luce...I've always considered you my daughter, just as much as Maisie. I know some people, usually those who dwell on everything, don't believe that I think this. It's not about belief. It is about knowing. I knew it the moment I first saw you. Whatever the future holds, I'll always be there for you."

"Thanks, Dad." I say looking up at him.

Nav

Lucie arrives in London and I call to see how she is doing. I could have messaged her, but I want to hear her voice and know that she is okay. I want to arrange to come down and see her at Central Saint Martins. I miss our conversations about everything and anything; it isn't quite the same chatting with Archie. I catch her at a bad moment, or so she says. Apparently she's busy in a workshop induction, learning how to screen-print her latest fabric design. "I'll call you back later," she says.

Lucie

I really mean to call Nav back. The design is the one I'd started over the summer; shapes and colours inspired by the Punjabi wall hanging his mother gave me. The Phulkari is displayed on the wall of my plain room in halls alongside one of Mum's hand-printed black and white film photographs of the marsh, of home.

I finally return Nav's call at the start of October. I can't quite believe that I've left it so long. We've exchanged messages, but never quite found the time to speak; both of us so caught up in the whirlwind of Freshers Week and a heavy workload.

Nav

It is after a lecture that I take Lucie's call whilst walking along the banks of the Cam. Her voice and the riverside setting takes me right back to the day we'd sat by the river and eaten *pakora*. I miss my friends from home, but the pressure is on, and I need to study.

After that conversation Lucie and I message each other most days.

Lucie

Nav and I sustain a forty-day Snapchat streak until often too tired, too hungover and too busy with end of term deadlines I simply forget.

Nav

I focus on work as the term gains pace. I am amongst people equally as bright and clever as me. It comes as a bit of a shock. I have to work hard to up my game. The promised trip to London to see the Christmas lights and ice skate against the backdrop of the Natural History Museum never happens.

Christmas comes. Our family take an extended break and visit relatives in Gojra and Karachi.

Lucie

I have a pleasant Christmas at home, returning to London for New Year's Eve on Primrose Hill, watching fireworks of the city with my art school friends and my new boyfriend, Thor. He's so warm and fun to be with. Everyone loves Thor, who is from Copenhagen and studying here.

Pictures of Nav with family and his mates, some of whom have become my (online) friends too, deluge my feed from early evening, for in Pakistan it is already New Year.

By January there are so many other pulls on my time that the messages to Nav grow sporadic. Occasionally, though, late at night, working on an essay I wonder what Nav would say about a piece of art theory. I send him messages and voice notes. I miss seeing these things through his eyes. His replies are always intriguing and spur me on with my studies.

Increasingly, I wonder what Hanif would say about my designs and growing interest in connections between Eastern and Western art. Would he be proud of his daughter going to art school, just as he'd always hoped to do?

Nav

Occasionally, I look at a painting, a view over the Cam, a piece of fabric on Cambridge Market, or a display of street food and take a photograph, which I send to Lucie.

2017-2018

Second Year at University

Nav

Finally, through the ticket barrier, I run towards platform 5b and the train to Norwich. There is a crowd on the platform, but no train. "The 17.59 train to Norwich is cancelled due to animals on the line. Please take the first train to London Liverpool Street for an onward connection to Norwich."

A groan goes out and then there's a mad rush over the footbridge for the waiting train to London. I am disappointed, not just that the journey is going to take an extra hour, but that I will miss out on going through Ely station where I always like to look out for the DB Cargo Class 666 and Freightliner class 60. I know, too much detail, but I love watching the coloured containers that have travelled so many miles, continuing their journey. The same kind of magic I feel when gazing at a map or a globe. I'm not the only one entranced by this. There's usually a whole crowd of train spotters at Ely junction.

I take a window seat. I always love a window seat on a train.

"Honestly," says the grey-haired woman sitting down next to me and wedging an enormous suitcase in beside her, "cancelling trains due to animals on the line."

"It's usually cows on the Cambridge to Norwich route."

"Whatever next?" she chuckles.

"There was a deer on the line when I went home for Christmas. It went right into the train."

"Spare me the details."

"That's Norfolk for you," I say, realising how much I've missed home. I am looking forward to the weekend, even if it is just for a few days for my sister, Nadiya's birthday. I take out my latest copy of *National Geographic* and pull my baseball cap down and hide away in my own world. I pause at a feature, headlined: *In the 21st century we are all migrants.* I read on, *we are all migrants across geography and time.* I think of my own family spread across three continents. *All of us are descended from those who left the Rift Valley in Africa.*

I drift off into a semi-conscious dreamlike state and think of home. I think of Lucie, probably because she was so bothered by the question: Where are you *really* from? The real answer to this question connects us all: we're all originally from Africa. When I get a phone signal, I'll text her and tell her this.

Lucie

"You sure you don't want a pudding?" asks Uncle Nabeel. I shake my head.

"I'll miss my train if I do," I say. He beckons the waitress over and asks for the bill. I've eaten every morsel of a very tasty aubergine stew at one of the restaurants just outside Liverpool Street Station. Uncle Nabeel has some business interests in the area and he often takes me out for a meal, where we talk about many things. Today I told him about how Mum and Dad have started working together in the wedding photography business. It's going from strength to strength, turning out to be more lucrative than teaching or building. He laughed when I explained that there was a bit of a blip when Dad started offering bespoke wedding cakes. I might love Dad's quirky designs, but they were a bit too much for the conventional wedding customers.

The first time Uncle Nabeel invited me to meet in London he apologised for staring at me that day when I came in to collect my portfolio. "The way you held yourself, the frown, the eyes. It was like seeing a ghost, the ghost of my brother," he said. Nabeel also told me how proud he was that someone in the family was involved in textiles after the necessary move into property.

I've also got to know his wife, Leila. A couple of months ago I visited them in their fancy Birmingham home. Uncle Nabeel sent a driver to collect me from New Street station. The driver proudly informed me that a famous footballer lived next door to my relatives. Uncle Nabeel wasn't home; he'd been called away at the last minute on some important business matter, so it fell to Aunty Leila to host me. She served green tea and sweet pastries. Aunty Leila's lack of English and my lack of Punjabi, and no Uncle Nabeel on hand to translate initially made for an awkward conversation. That day was the start of me teaching her English. At first it was simple conversation and then we were soon on to reading and writing. I especially liked it when she wrote out recipes for me to try and make. I can serve chapati from scratch on a curry night! In return for the English lessons Aunty Leila taught me traditional Punjabi embroidery. The conversations we have sewing together are radically changing my ideas about art.

We all have those moments when the course of our lives can spin on a pin. Learning about my Punjabi textile heritage was one of them. And of course, that morning, when I spat into the test tube and sent off my DNA, to find out where I was *really* from, but that seems like a lifetime ago. Everything you think you know can change in an instant.

I thought that the answer would lead me far and wide, and in some ways it has; but its within myself that I have started to feel most whole and grounded. These days, wherever I am, I am proud to be me.

Maisie would probably laugh at such a notion. Or say, "You always over think everything!" But she too had her moment where everything changed. It was exactly the same moment that Nav's face paled at the mention of his mother being my half-sister. Some people might even call it synchronicity. I can even prove the timings. I've kept the message.

> Maisie: You'll never believe it. I'm signed up on the plumbing BTEC. The only girl!

She finishes her course this summer and has plans for her own business: *Girls on Tap*.

Mum and I, and then Mum and Dad, had their own difficult discussion about my father and then it was never openly mentioned again, except that day Dad drove me down to London. Not because anyone wanted to sweep things under the carpet, but because there was nothing more to add. And we all felt a strange kind of closure.

"Good to hear that you are all well," says Uncle Nabeel. "You'd better go before you miss your train."

"Thanks for dinner," I say, picking up my overnight bag and power walking across Broadgate and into the station, praying I'll make the 19.30 train to Norwich.

I check the departure board. The next train to Norwich is in two minutes. I rush down to platform nine. At the ticket barrier, with just over a minute to go, a tall man in a T-shirt and baseball cap struggles to get an enormous suitcase through the gate. Beside him is an older woman in a bright floral print dress. They are blocking the ticket barrier. My heart is pounding. I'm going to miss the train if they don't get a move on!

The man finally clears the barrier. I follow him, the woman and suitcase onto the end carriage. The doors bang shut. The whistle blows. Down the aisle and looking for a vacant seat we all go. The next-but-one carriage is the buffet car. The woman and case go to sit at a table. The man in the cap joins the queue. I'm desperate for a cold drink and stand in line.

The train picks up pace. The man takes off his cap and stuffs it into his pocket. He uses the adjacent window as a mirror and smoothes down his jet-black hair. The train judders, he turns. His eyes meet mine. The train rattles on. A mother and child push past us.

"I don't believe it!" he says. There's a long moment when we don't know whether to kiss, hug or to shake hands.

"Going home for the weekend?" says Nav.

I nod. "Yep!"

"Me too. It's Nadiya's birthday."

"Next please," says the steward.

"What can I get you?" asks Nav.

"A sparkling water, please."

"One sparkling water and one coffee. Black, no milk, unless you have soya or oat milk?" says Nav.

The steward looks at him as if he's asked for champagne.

"Black is fine," says Nav.

"Synchronicity or what?" I say. "I've just had dinner with our uncle." I stop myself from saying anymore about the psychological concept that events are "meaningful coincidences" if they occur with no causal relationship, yet seem to be meaningfully related. Nav would probably call it pseudo-science! But it happens all the time: you think about someone and then you spot them across the street, or your phone rings and it's them. I remember the day we bumped into each other and I dropped my phone. I remember the way this coincidence set off a whole chain of events which led to finding the answer to my burning question: Where am I *really* from? That was synchronicity.

Nav takes the drinks and turns to me. "I'm not sure I believe in synchronicity, but you won't believe it, I was reading an article on the train and was about to message you about it. But I can tell you in person now."

2018-2019

Third Year at University

Lucie

I can't believe that my artwork is actually up on display for the world to see. Three years of study all leading to this day, and the private view is tonight. It has taken several days to work out how best to display my textile designs and the accompanying film. I stand back and take in the exhibition.

Roisin, my tutor, walks around the show pinning up our names and artist statements. "Looking good," she says.

"I'm still not sure whether *Punjab to Paisley* should be the first piece viewers see."

"It's always hard with a series. But I think you've made the right decision. The video definitely works better away from the other pieces. You have to believe in your work, your vision, and stand by your choices," she says.

"I know," I sigh.

"Think of it as first night nerves. There's always going to be people who love, and people who hate any artistic creation. The main thing is that you have something important to say and it will move people."

"It's just so personal. It's hard to separate *me* from the work."

"Lucie. That isn't a bad thing. I think you're done here, anything more and you'll be overthinking it. Go home and get changed," she says. "As long as you're back just before six, all will be okay."

London is busy. I head down the escalator into the underground. The heat and stale, stuffy air of the Northern line is worse than ever. I need a shower and to make myself presentable for the private gallery viewing. Hopefully Jenny and Clara—our new flatmate—will be home and we can get ready and make our way to the show together.

We rattle through the tunnel. This is the first moment I've had to sit and properly think about tonight. I'm nervous about my very first private view. It's like inviting people to your birthday party and hoping they will come and have a good time. Almost everyone has said they'll be at Central Saint Martins tonight: Mum, Dad, Maisie and even Nana Pat. Plus the other side of my family are coming: Aunty Maryam and Uncle Maneer—without the kids for a mini break in London. Uncle Nabeel and Aunty Leila are coming too. And of course my biological father, Hanif, who so desperately wanted to go to art school himself, is an ethereal presence in my work. The only person who can't make it is Nav. I completely understand why. He is miles away in Chicago. He finally summoned up the courage to take a gap year from his studies. He's going to return to Cambridge in October for his final year and get his degree. Yet, without Nav I would never have created this show.

Nav

The Heathrow express draws into Paddington Station. I'm first off and out onto the concourse. After the air-conditioned train it is like stepping into an oven! It is rush hour and office workers in summer dresses and short-sleeved shirts brush past me knocking into my enormous rucksack. The old-fashioned station clock hands are pointing towards six. No time to take the bus, or even see if there's an Uber driver in the vicinity. I sprint outside and hail a black cab.

"Where are you going, mate?" asks the driver.

"Central Saint Martins Art School," I say, wedging my rucksack in beside me.

"Coal Drops Yard?"

I nod. We queue at the traffic lights. "Been on a trip, have we?"

"Chicago," I confirm. "I was there on a student work away scheme."

"Wow! Lucky for some," he says as we drive off.

Lucie

Nav's family are already here. His Mum and Dad are dressed in their smart casuals. Uncle Nabeel wears jeans and a T-shirt, the way the super-rich often ignore dress codes, and Aunty Leila is in a beautiful green shalwar kameez decorated with gold trim. "I'll see you all upstairs," I say, going to look for Mum and Dad.

I wait outside by the cool of the fountains. Kids run in and out of the numerous spurting water jets. For a moment I wish I could join them. But there they are! Mum and Dad are leading the way across the square, and slowly bringing up the rear is Nana Pat clasping tightly onto Maisie's arm. They are chatting away whilst Maisie is using her free hand to navigate with her phone. They haven't seen me yet.

I like observing them. After all, isn't an artist someone who notices things? Mum and Dad make for a handsome couple and seem so very different away from home. Mum is wearing black trainers and a calf-length dress. Very fashionable! And thank goodness Dad isn't in his blue boiler suit! He's wearing smart navy-blue trousers and a crisp white shirt. They're dressed up as if they're going to a wedding!

I wave. They finally see me.

"Lucie!" calls Dad.

"We're here at last," says Mum.

We hug and I lead them towards the art school. "It must have been a major job turning this old industrial site into an art school, shops and cafes," says Dad gazing around.

"Back in my day these old warehouses were where everyone flocked to rave parties," says Mum.

"You went to raves?" asks Maisie.

Mum shrugs. "I was young once."

"Drink, anyone?" I ask, leading them over to the pop-up bar.

Mum takes a plastic cup of warm white wine and passes one to Nana. Dad and Maisie help themselves to a couple of beers. "An end-of-course degree show is a much better way to celebrate all your hard work than those boring old graduation ceremonies." Mum gazes around the exhibition. "This takes me back to my end-of-year show."

"Like mother, like daughter," Dad says smiling.

And also like my other dad, I think, but decide not to share this. I suddenly feel nervous as to how my family is going to react to my exhibition. I'll find that out soon enough when we go upstairs. Should I have discussed my ideas more with Mum? Maybe I should have told her about the day I spent at the *Time Out* archive and that moment when I found the photographs she'd taken of my father, Hanif. The ones she didn't think they'd publish. I wanted to digest and use that information without Mum's influence, yet now I feel I should have warned her.

Don't worry about other people's opinions, I tell myself. Nav and I have discussed it and he really gets my ideas. We've messaged each other so many times over the last few months. His comments and the way his scientific brain works made my dissertation so much better. I wish he was here to see the show.

Nav

The taxi stops and starts as we crawl past Regent's Park. People are relaxing on the grass. We are overtaken by scooters and bikes, even pedestrians are going quicker than us. If I didn't have such a big bag, I'd get out and run.

"Don't worry, I know a shortcut," says the driver as if he's reading my mind. He swerves down a back street and starts telling me about how he had to memorise the streets of London to pass his taxi driver exam.

"A bit like swotting for University Challenge," I say. "I was on Peterhouse's team last year. I memorised all the Chinese dynasties and knew the Periodic Table by rote anyway."

"I'll have to watch that on catch-up," says the driver smiling widely through the intermediary of the rear-view mirror. "You're a celeb, mate."

We pull up outside the art school. I pay and jump out of the taxi. I scroll down my phone looking for the email, after all a private view is by invitation only. I step into the packed foyer. Nobody is checking invites. I'm boiling hot and want to take my jacket off, but am unsure where to put it, or my rucksack. They don't seem to have cloakrooms like in an actual gallery.

More importantly I need a drink. I head over to the bar. I dip my hand in the bowl of bottles which circle like torpedo boats in melting ice floes as if I'm at a lucky dip. I pull out a bottle of beer. I put it straight back in.

The girl behind the bar watches me. "Do you have any soft drinks?" I ask.

"Sure. Orangeade or elderflower?"

"Can I have both please?" I ask.

The girl smiles.

"I've had a long journey," I say, gazing down at my backpack.

She hands me a plastic cup of elderflower cordial and takes a can of orangeade from the cool box. "Do you want me to look after that bag?" she asks eyeing the rucksack. "You don't want to damage any of the artworks. I can store it under the table."

"Thanks," I say, sliding my bag under the bar. I down my drinks. *Where exactly is Lucie's exhibition?* It suddenly dawns on me that I haven't told anyone, not even my parents that I changed my flight home so I could be at Lucie's private view. I wanted to keep it as a surprise. I message Lucie.

> Nav: Hiya Lucie. I'm here.

> Lucie: What do you mean, here?

> Nav: In the foyer. At the bar. Where do I go? Where are you?

> Lucie: Wow! I can't believe you're here. Wait there, I'm coming to get you right now.

Lucie is wearing a summer dress that resembles a wall of Turkish tiles. She runs over and gives me the biggest of hugs. "I can't believe you're really here."

"Part of me is still halfway across the Atlantic and jet-lagged; but otherwise, I'm good."

"Come on upstairs. My work is on the first floor. Everyone is here."

"I've missed you." says Lucie.

"I've missed you too."

Lucie

At the far end of the room there is clinking on a glass. "*She* has a *real* wine glass," whispers Mum sipping from her plastic cup.

"Who is she?" asks Dad.

"The principal, Frances Ecke," I explain.

"When you're that important you get a real glass," laughs Dad.

Gradually the whole room comes to a hush. "We still haven't had a proper look at your work," says Mum.

"Later," I whisper.

"Good evening. Thank you, each and every one of you, for coming to see the work of this year's wonderfully talented Art and Design students." There's a long awkward pause in which the principal seems to have lost her place on the iPad. "I would like you to put your hands together for this year's graduates." Applause ricochets around the room and I wish Dad wouldn't clap quite so enthusiastically. Frances waits before continuing. "Our students have created such a diverse and challenging show. They were supported by many of you here this evening: our staff, family and friends." Cue another round of applause.

She goes on to list awards for architecture, ceramics, communication design, fashion design, furniture design, and graphic design. Next up is textile design. My heart is pounding. Part of me knows my work is good. *But is it good enough for a prize?*

"The award for textile design goes to Thor Raaby," she announces.

"Weren't you going out with him?" whispers Maisie.

"Yes," I hiss. "But that was ages ago." I'm not sure if I'm relieved or disappointed. Either way, after we split up, we became quite good friends. "His work is amazing. Very Danish with minimalist blocks of colour, even if it is inspired by Lego," I say.

"Nothing wrong with Lego," laughs Maisie.

The awards and clapping go on for a while longer and hopefully we're nearing the end. "And our final awards," says the principal taking a large sip of water, "are this year's Nova Prizes for exceptional work which challenges our understanding of their chosen art and design discipline. Our winners are from across different courses, and in no particular order are: Shane Batica, Kai Wong and Lucie Hansen."

"Lucie, it's you!" shrieks Maisie, nudging me in the ribs. My legs turn to jelly and I'm not sure I can walk the few metres across the floor to collect the envelope.

"Go on, Luce," says Nav.

I am beside my family clutching an envelope without quite knowing how I made it there and back.

"Let's go and have a proper look at Lucie's work," says Mum.

This is it. I am nervous. I want them to like the work, and more importantly I want them to understand why I made it.

We all gather round the textile hangings. Mum is the only one reading my artist statement.

WHERE ARE YOU *REALLY* FROM?

Lucie Hansen
BA Textile Design

The work combines traditions from Eastern and Western art, from the artist's British-Asian cultural heritage, identity and experience. Art, craft and research is at the heart of this collection titled: Where are you *really* from?

The artist immersed herself in her family's textile history from the Punjab and East Anglia. The six hangings take elements from Norfolk shawl Paisley designs and Punjabi floral and geometric Phulkari motifs. They are combined with English words inherited from the Indian subcontinent. The words dungarees, bandana, gingham, chintz, calico, and pyjamas are scattered amongst imagery in the form of word play.

The work is informed by historical archival material from diverse sources, such as: the Norfolk Museums Service and the Time Out Group magazine archive.

Materials

Six digital fabric artworks are displayed on light boxes, with each one highlighting a different theme relating to the textile heritage of Britain and the Indian subcontinent.

The fabric is of building quality, so it is strong and fireproof. Hand and digital painting and printing processes are combined, before being printed on a roll and stretched over light boxes. This process allows for striking complementary colour schemes, such as; indigo and gold, and rose-red and green.

The illuminated hangings resemble stained glass and are framed in an oriental carpet style border.

An accompanying short film plays out on a loop. The zoomed-in fingers in the first part are members of the artist's family: crafting a cake, taking a photograph, sketching, embroidering and cross-stitching. These film and still images are collaged and overlaid as a visual mechanism to tell the artist's own story. The final frames point to a global narrative, where hands from around the world share the joy of making.

My family gather around the show. Jenny and Clara see the little crowd and join us. They are followed by my tutor. "Well done! Most deserved," says Roisin.

"Speech! Speech!" says Maisie.

"I don't do speeches."

"Go on," presses Maisie. "Tell us all about it."

I step nervously towards my work. "I'll keep it short," I say. I take a deep breath. "Thank you for coming tonight. Some of you have travelled a long way." I smile at Nav. "Some of you have travelled further than you have for a long time." Nana Pat wipes away a tear. "This show, this art wouldn't be possible without each and every one of you. The pieces are about all of us."

"This is like the Oscars," says Jenny in a stage whisper to Mum.

"Where are you *really* from? is the title of this collection, my show and my dissertation. It is the question which bugged me for so long. Over the last few years, I began to consider myself to be half-British and half-Pakistani. I explained this to my tutor, Roisin Patel."

Mum's eyes fill with tears—which makes my eyes fill up too. I can't speak.

"And I said," interjects Roisin, "you're not half anything. Saying you are half just relegates you to not being good enough. You are British *and* you are Pakistani. Just as I am Irish and Gujarati. We are global citizens. You are also a fantastic artist and designer, a daughter, a grand-daughter, sister, cousin, niece, friend." She looks over to me, as if to say, "Lucie, carry on."

"I thought my project was complete with the textile hangings; that was until I discussed the ideas with my cousin, Nav. He reminded me of a conversation we had a while back on the train up to Norwich about how through DNA we are all connected. This was the inspiration for the film. The video piece explores the connectedness of those of us who make things by hand, from my closest relatives to people from all over the world." I take a theatrical bow. "I'll leave the work to do the talking,"

I walk over to Mum. She is standing beside Maryam and Nabeel. The three of them are transfixed by the camera panning across Hanif's face. "Lucie, you tracked down those old photographs! I thought they were lost to time," says Mum.

"It was as if Hanif was wiped from our family history, and now you've brought him back to us in so many ways," says Maryam turning to me.

Nabeel sighs deeply. He watches the film in silence.

The camera zooms in on Hanif's eyes and on to my hands turning the pages of his sketchbook. Quick drawings of people striding across a park, followed by intricate studies of trees fill the screen. When I first came across the sketchbooks he'd kept as a teenager at home in Birmingham, it felt magical touching something he had touched. A direct link with my father. The drawings were like a diary letting me into his world. Little details of everyday life recorded in pages of exquisite drawings of people and places.

Mum puts her arm around my shoulder. "Well done!" she says. "I'm so proud of you. You know, he would have been completely amazed by your work."

"Oh Mum," I say. "That means so much. I thought you might be angry that I didn't let on about the lost photographs until tonight."

"It's all part of the creative process. I understand. I love the way you filmed the turning of sketchbook pages to bring his drawings back to life. And then the panning across the old black and white photographs turning the prints into moving images was genius," says Mum, forever the photography lecturer.

Dad gives me a squeeze and a proud smile.

"Let's all go for dinner. I've booked us a table just round the corner. Dinner is on me!" booms Uncle Nabeel, back to his normal lively self and trying to organise us all!

We walk out into the warm night. "So what next?" asks Uncle Nabeel.

"I need to try and sell some of my work, to make a living as a textile artist and designer."

"Thought so. I have a proposition for you."

Uncle Nabeel tells me he is developing some of the old warehouses round the corner from here and plans to turn it into a carbon neutral creative hub. "It will be one of the biggest developments in Europe, full of artists, designers and makers," he says excitedly. "Artists and entrepreneurs aren't so different from each other. We think outside the box and envisage a different future."

"That sounds amazing," I say.

"You can have a studio there rent free for a year. Just to get you started."

"But I want to pay my own way."

"You'd be doing *me* a favour," he says. "Once you are in, others will come."

Nav runs along and catches me up. "I loved the way your work showcased all those things we talked about, and in such a beautiful way."

"Thank you!"

"Almost as beautiful as the workings out of a complex equation."

"Almost?" I ask, smiling at my cousin.

I Am My Ancestors Dream

Your ancestors did not survive
everything that nearly ended them
for you to shrink yourself
to make someone else
comfortable.

This sacrifice is your war cry,
be loud,
be everything
and make them proud.

                                        Nikita Gill

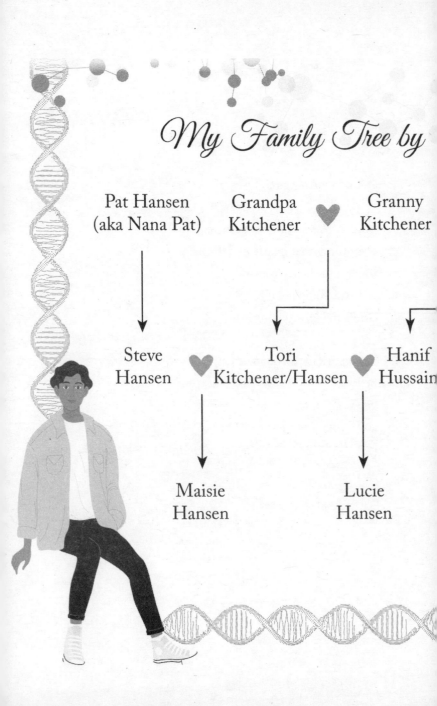

My Family Tree by

Pat Hansen (aka Nana Pat)

Grandpa Kitchener 💜 Granny Kitchener

Steve Hansen 💜 Tori Kitchener/Hansen 💜 Hanif Hussain

Maisie Hansen

Lucie Hansen

Lucie Hansen, aged 18

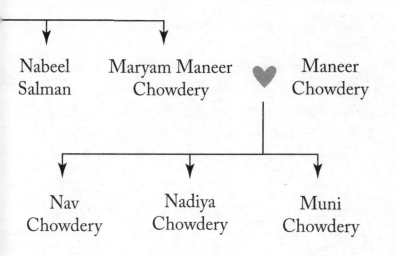

Nabeel Salman	Maryam Maneer Chowdery	♥	Maneer Chowdery

Nav Chowdery	Nadiya Chowdery	Muni Chowdery

Postscript

When I began writing this book it was in many ways a response to receiving the results of my own DNA test and an exploration of the question I've always been asked: Where are you *really* from? I did not know how I would feel finding out the results, and to anyone thinking of doing this, I suggest talking it through with experts before embarking on the journey.

What I do know is, we need better stories around living as a mixed-race person. Writing for me has always been an exploration of a puzzle circling in my head. I am interested in nature/nurture and the debates around it and hope the characters in the story will give insight into these themes.

Amanda Addison

Acknowledgements

Special thanks to friends and authors for their support and reading early versions of the manuscript. Your comments were invaluable! Erin Bradshaw, Aisha Bushby, Bethan Dunlop, Mariam Issimdar, Sally-Anne Lomas, John Nicholson, Grace Ryding, Sarah Passingham, Bella Pearson, Qaisra Shahraz, Sophie Saunders and Rebecca Shields. A shout out too, to the team at Searchlight Book Awards (especially Kim and Lu) for listing *Where are you **really** from?* (the early working title for *Looking for Lucie*) in their selection of best chapter openings. Thank you to the amazing editorial team at Neem Tree Press for their care and attention in bringing this story to print. Finally, thank you, dear reader, for taking the time to listen to Lucie's story, although a work of fiction, it has many themes close to my heart.